From the Mourners' *Kaddish*

Exalted and hallowed be God's great name
in the world which God created, according to plan.
May God's majesty be revealed in the days of our lifetime
and the life of all Israel — speedily, imminently,
To which we say: **Amen.**

CONTENTS

1. First, a word from Geoff 1
2. Hirsch or Harris: same difference! 5
3. Rudamina, a tiny *shtetel* 9
4. The mystery that is Joe Daniels 16
5. Simchat Torah – an ending and a beginning 20
6. What to do with three bottles of vodka..27
7. This is not *Goldene Medina*, Harris 45
8. Shy? Mary Ellen, *shy?!!!* 52
9. Simon Israel: a lap dog with no tail to wag....................................64
10. Mother Love...68
11. Now I prefer a pint and a pipe of St Bruno..................................86
12. It's a long way to 'Eureka' 93
13. Maurice or Harold: same difference! 107
14. Beyond the Pale..117
15. Hull: deep and muddy, but land nevertheless 121
16. Call me by a name, any name you like....................................... 126
17. A last word, perhaps 136
ABOUT THE AUTHOR 139
ACKNOWLEDGEMENTS.. 140

To Simon Israel Karavitch, whom I never met but wish I had.

1

First, a word from Geoff

Geoffrey, Godfrey, Ceolfrith – Anglo-Saxon for 'god-fearing' (or in Geoff's case, more probably the anglicised name of a Hollywood star of Westerns, who had grey sideburns)

Did he fear God?

In what sense fear, you should ask?

No cowering, guilt-ridden angst

for sure:

But a curious respect, a questioning reflection,

the passion of a kingdom built on justice.

And more than the occasional hint of love.

If that is 'fear' he could claim the name.

Sometimes.

This story struggles to find a beginning. Perhaps it started in the old Russian Empire or modern-day Lithuania, Dublin, Belfast, or more definitely in Manchester. Each country plays its part and could make a case for itself. Perhaps it started with a falling in love, or worse, a persecution or, at least, an enforced separation. Like all stories it has manifold events, as well as a few mysteries, but there again so does life. And, for all its players, in truth what went before is lost, at least for now, and the ending... well, that has still to be written. But even incomplete stories can be told.

Finding himself retired was a shock to Geoff's system. In a sense, he didn't feel that old, that is until he looked in the mirror, or saw his grown-up son making the same ridiculous mistakes that he had years before. Time is like that: it ticks away when you are most distracted. Soon enough you have to catch up with it, but it can be a shocking experience *en route*. It's not just the wrinkles, the aches and moans, the afternoon naps or the endless discussions about medicine and ailments that are the tell-tale signs that the years have advanced while you were not looking. The truth is that you are just beginning to notice what has been happening to you, all the time. There are more subtle hints. Those moments you speak and your dad comes out of your mouth. The feeling of being just slightly out of touch, and worse, the memory of lost opportunities and aborted adventures.

Above all, Geoff became more and more curious about his roots, as if to forget what had gone before him was to allow it all to slip away. Lately, he had all too easily found himself wallowing in nostalgia, trying to recall the names of school friends, or neighbours in the street of his boyhood capers. He could laugh out loud at the characters who had long since passed through his life, leaving traces, vestiges of their lives, permanently attached to him. Yet he reflected he had long since lost any real-time contact with them or their lives. Old family photographs merely added to the developing hinterland of, so far, unrecorded memories. However, what perturbed him most, what teased his thoughts in those sleepless pillow moments, was a deeper question: how did he come to be, well, *him?* What influences, experiences outside of his recall, what murky family history or unrevealed gene swamp, had bubbled up to produce little (quite literally, and on both counts) old him? Was he merely a product of his known, and unknown, past? A reincarnation of an equally flawed predecessor if you like, or at best, an evolved development of history? Were there other Geoff Millers in times gone by, who had lived and struggled with similar lives, displayed the same traits, characteristics or emotions, long before he burst from his mother's womb on that snowy day in January '56? In short, he became preoccupied with his roots – the deepest ones, those long since relegated to the secret, unrevealed world of his own personal history. Who was he and how had he come about? *'Who cares?'* you may sensibly ask. He certainly did (and does), often. The more he searched, the bigger the hinterland became, and the more insignificant one ruminant, aging individual seemed to become. Yet he continued to care. Life was puzzling, especially with so many pieces missing and that incompleteness disrupted him, especially in the early hours of the morning after a little too much red wine. In his defence, not just for himself, but for those who followed, those who carried on the line, so to speak. What had he deposited on them, *in* them even? So, began a time of human archaeology, if you like. It is a popular pastime with the retired. He imagined a whole army of grey-haired, wrinkled retired folk spending hours trawling internet sites on their computers, searching for glimpses of a past they had long since lost. Hours of wasted electricity and used gigabytes of data, trying to find past names and people, their hatches, matches and despatches.

Amazement at unearthed family members and lists of children read out with *'ooh-ahs'* and excited cooing and giggles. Though he had some unfounded notion that, unlike others, he was finding more than dates and names and connections, but real roots. Roots that mattered. He was fascinated by some of those factors (dates and names) to be sure, but he was convinced that we are more than the sum of simple biographical data. He was more concerned with mysteries, the minutia of lives and, most of all, mega changes, moments of familial paradigm shifts, traces of how he had evolved. To satisfy such a curiosity would need more than bare facts, and would, without doubt, like the attraction of a strong magnet, draw him to Joe Daniels. Who was Joe Daniels and what part does Joe Daniels have in his, and his family's, formation? A question that had been asked by others, as well as himself, but a question that so far eluded any answers.

2

Hirsch or Harris: same difference!

Hirsch – the gazelle: a symbol of grace and beauty

Light of foot, fast, slim, even elegant.
Preferring the background; nimble enough to silently retreat
and find the green foliage, that hides the beauty within.
No flamboyant figure, instead graceful, wide-eyed reflection.
Moving steadily, softly aware, watching,
chewing on life.

Hirsch knew in his blood what was happening. He had learnt to read the runes with remarkable ease; he saw the writing on the wall. Though it seemed impossible to get any worse, there was bad news in the air. He could smell it, feel it, almost touch it, and with it there was the rising of an age-old fear. A fear that his family, and his people, had known so many times. Nothing startling in that; most of his friends and peers had already reached the same conclusion. People (who are they?) say history repeats itself and that was something his own people didn't need reminding off. They (his people) often hoped that they would escape their turn, but knew in their deepest thoughts that it was unlikely. They tried, in a thousand and one ways, to dodge the inevitable onslaught. Who wouldn't? Some converted to Christianity, (Catholic or Orthodox, same difference), others changed their names to be less obvious. They built reputations, good businesses and they stored up treasures, not simply to help the local economy, but to store up treasure that they could easily transport if it proved necessary. They stayed in crowds wherever they could; at least, they thought, there may be more safety among the herd. But in reality, whatever they did, they remained outsiders. They ate differently, they looked different, they 'did' differently, and so they were inevitably confined to life on the edges. So, they created their own infrastructures, mechanisms, whole economies, and practices. A sub-culture if you would, their own distinctive way of life. Yet in the end they were always dependent on the goodwill of the authorities. And that goodwill was often in short supply! They were Jews after all!

Rudamina had its own Jewish butchers, doctors, schools, all organised through the synagogue. The doctor, Eli Cohen, had grown up with their father, and Mordecai, the butcher's family, had provided their meat in their kosher way for generations. Now, deep in his gut, Hirsch could feel that the worm was turning again, as he, along with his friends and neighbours, watched nervously and waited for the inevitable signs, the mist of threat to turn into menacing actions. They tried to keep one step ahead. It was crucial to know if and when to move on, the right time to pick up sticks,

sticks with which to hit out or lean on and limp off to another place and try again. They needed to know when they dare not stay any longer, for their family's safety, for their safety, for the future they yearned for, but a future of which they were so often deprived. He had learnt to live, or was it *exist*, in a place of liminal anxiety. It was a life. A life that got harder with each new responsibility. His father taught him about remaining detached, keeping relationships to the minimum. In short, never to cling; instead, to 'let loose and let fly' as the saying goes. Jews had practised the art over the years. Accomplished players, they chose portable ways of living, ready to pack up and move on at the drop of a proverbial hat. For the lucky, such portability was achieved by working with gold or diamonds, for others having an expertise that travels, and goods that are easily stowed for the journey.

However, 'the simple people of scissors and ironing board' was what they called the likes of Hirsch Karavitch. For him and his people, poor and struggling to eke out a living, scissors became the tools of their trade, along with cotton and needles and a hot iron and board. The 'tools of the trade' only needed a small bag. People always needed clothes and Hirsch the tailor could provide them. Like his father and grandfather, he was one of the many tailors in Rudamina. Hopefully, he could continue to make a living and feed the hungry mouths of a quiver of little ones! But there was no shortage of tailors in the neighbourhood, so making a real living was no easy task. A better future seemed an impossible dream. Thank G-d for the Relief Fund which they relied on just to get through some weeks.

Looking back, it's hard to pinpoint how and when he knew things were really starting to turn sour. It happened slowly, tick by tick of the clock, or like snowflakes lightly falling at the start of the storm. But the clouds darkened, the danger signals continued to add up. Tiny things at first: the news reports with innuendos, the rumours of trouble-rousing, slurs that they, the Jews, were job-pinching, accusations of his people taking over, swarms of 'dirty Jews', they called them. Then the breakouts of incidents, muggings, cruel words spoken as 'jokes' or less subtly spoken to degrade, graffiti daubed on their shops or an occasional mysterious fire that damaged the wooden shacks. Misinformation and terrible scapegoating followed and they were often blamed falsely for hideous crimes. Remember the time they were accused of kidnappings and murdering goy children? No wonder people hated them if they believed such abhorrent lies! One bad apple was bad news for them all. One cheating Jew, one demanding money lender, one trickster with some cards and it let the bad blood. It fanned the burning flames of wicked rumours. Poverty among them deepened and sharpened. Queues of unemployed Jews seeking relief from hard-pressed charities, threatened religious leaders frightened of losing their grip. All of these, and more, were the usual precursors to the inevitable, deliberate terrors and attacks. A demonising of 'them' steadily developed; at worse, they were made out to be less than human, vermin even. If they hadn't left by then, who knows what might have become of them? How do you treat vermin? His people knew too many examples of the horrors that would be mercilessly dealt out. So, there were two simple age-old options: fight or flight. To be fair, maybe there was a third – to ignore it all, put your head down and hope that the tide would change. But sadly, history proved it rarely did.

3
Rudamina, a tiny *shtetel*

Rudamina – a tributary

Not all names have meanings.
Some meanings are lost in the past.
Names locate, pinpoint places or persons, times, virtues, crafts.
Sometimes they hint at identity, sometimes elusive, hidden in distant history.
But wherever a river flows, it bursts life.

Among the vast expanse and beauty of the lake district of Lazdijai, not far from the present-day border with Poland to the west and larger provincial town of Kaunas (formally Kovno) to the East, lies what is left of the Lithuanian village of Rudamina, or Rudamin. Though its origins went back to the sixteenth century, it was later, in 1750, that the Princess Gawronski invited Jews to come to the town. At first, mainly tailors and shoemakers settled there. A rabbi arrived later and made his living from an inn. They built a prayer house, they leased a field for the cemetery, and Jewish life began to develop, thrive even. Sadly, it was short-lived; soon, Jews were ridiculed and persecuted, even refused use of the water from the river Rudaminelis that flowed through the town. The numbers diminished; they left for safer places or the hope of sanctuary. That all changed again when at the end of the century one Jew bought the entire town. So Rudamina prospered as a centre of Jewish life again. In the small *shtetel*, Jewish families lived a healthy, productive, independent life with a distinctly Jewish identity. In the middle of the nineteenth century, among the tailors in the town was Hirsch (or later Harris) Karavitch. Faced with the decision to stay or to leave, he would never know that the consequences of his choice would be way beyond his worse expectations or cruellest imagination.

*

Hirsch wasn't really aware of when the Karavitch family had first arrived in Rudamina. It was long before he was around, for sure. The truth is, he knew nowhere else. Kinsfolk spread around the local neighbourhoods, though never too far; they were a large family after all. Jews are townsfolk and most lived near enough to the synagogue, even if they were not great attenders. And it was a good job because they relied on family, they were too exposed in the country villages. Jewish families 'knew people who could' and that was a different kind of safety. But large numbers, as well as providing a feeling of security, conversely also spelt threat to others. The Jewish dilemma – together we stand but together we make a pretty easy target. He couldn't honestly say that he never thought about, never mind understood, what went on in the minds of the Gentiles around him or those who had power over him and his like. He couldn't easily say why they disliked his people so much. It was just as it was, as it always had been. He was used to living on the edges of their society. For him, though, life was about survival each and every day. It exercised all his energy. How could he make a little money here or there, buy food and shelter, get on with a life without feeling scared for his family or for himself?

Tailors were two a penny in the *shtetel* but he managed to find enough work to get by. Just! There were at least three tailors on Schneider Street. And all next to each other. Tailors were among the poorest paid. His workshop, if that was what you were brave enough to call it, really belonged to Chaim, his father's older brother. It was on the corner of Bolshaya Street and Schneider Street, and both led into the little market square. 'Good for business,' Chaim said, and on the edge of the neighbourhood, too. That was a boost. Strange to have a market place on the edge of a town but *goyim* didn't like to travel much into the Jewish neighbourhood except to rampage. They were also near enough to do good business in Suwałki – a trek away but not impossible and with a much larger population. Even then, theirs was a tiny enterprise which often felt overshadowed by bigger shops nearby.

Hirsch once heard a joke about three tailors' shops next door to each other. The grandest had a sign above which read: 'The Famous Tailor's Shop of Kovno'; the next shop along, a smaller shop, had a bigger sign which read: 'The Best Tailors of Kovno'; and the third, at the end, a much smaller and less lugubrious shop, had a sign above its door which read: 'The Tailors of Kovno, MAIN ENTRANCE'. He suggested the idea to his uncle but he didn't see the funny side. At least not on that day.

*

Rudamina was a glum, grey village, little more than a settlement of wooden shacks, though each plot had a proudly fenced boundary. The plots were big enough to keep a few hens and an odd sheep.

There weren't many more streets in the *shtetel*: Jatkower Street where the butchers slaughtered and sold the kosher meat, and Pylimo Street that led to the old fort. The fort was the most famous landmark of the village, though for now it lay unused. The streets were little more than dirt tracks. Wooden boards marked the edges, acting as pavements to keep feet out of the mud on the many rainy days that drenched the place. Horse and cart were the usual transport, though walking worked well, given the size of the *shtetel*. Provided, that is, you could dodge the mud. A pretty basic inn sat at the centre. Built by Rabbi Svirsky, it provided him with an income, and the synagogue met in a downstairs room. It was the centre of village life. That was in the early days, of course. One day there would be other synagogues and other rabbi *schule* for the children, and the earliest signs of what would become a dispensary and hospital. Later, there would even be a music hall of sorts but not in time for Hirsch to enjoy.

The Karavitch tailor shop was, in fact, not much more than a dark, drab room with ancient but (albeit only sometimes) working sewing machines around the walls, one for each of them. On old shelves that covered the walls batches of material were stacked on top of each other. Chaim was an expert at finding off-cuts and remnants, cloth with faults, that with clever cutting could be easily used. And, of course, he used old *goyim* clothes that could be reworked (sometimes completely) to fashion new garments for sale. They took commissions and, as the work developed, made their own stuff to sell on to local shops and families in the neighbouring *shtetels* and small towns. Cotton reels were stacked on spools and boxes, hundreds of boxes, with needles and buttons and tags. Paper patterns lay strewn around like discarded plans. An old table served as a cutting bench and two flat irons rested near to the old spitting boiler. Too little light, especially too little for old tired eyes, demanded the wearing of crude excuses for spectacles. Too cold in the winter and too hot in the summer, but, unlike an English suburban garden conservatory, this place was a veritable monument to the drudgery of daily life. To the untrained eye it was chaotic, a material mess, and it would be hard to believe anything creative could be made there. A smell of sweat, damp material, and burning oil hung around, amid the spluttering sound of the steam irons and old boiler. The *snip, snip* of scissors and, of course, the whirring of the wheels as pedals pressed and pressed like some syncopated background music of an old black and white movie trying forever to catch up the action. Not that those working there would notice as noses and ears became easily accustomed to their regular settings. They learned to block out, to accommodate or to accept with weary resignation the place that they inhabited. Four of them worked the machines: Isaac and Abraham, Chaim's beloved sons, and Hirsch and Woolf, their cousins. Family! Not that it was cosy: the boiler only managed to splutter a mean warmth and fingers covered in cheap fingerless gloves soon froze. Chaim drove a hard sweat from them all. Hard work was cheaper than putting more wood on the boiler! On occasions, he favoured his sons, understandable perhaps. Usually Abraham, the youngest, who was, in reality, least likely to deliver good finished products, was the most favoured. I guess that's the youngest's privilege. But Hirsch made a living, a poor one, just enough to feed his growing household.

Hirsch married Rosa in '86. It was a small affair, held, of course, at the synagogue. The rabbi directed the rite and, as Hirsch smashed a glass under his feet, he knew only too well that the future would have its own pain and crisis. He already knew Rosa's family, the Schimanskis, but until the marriage was arranged he hardly knew Rosa. That was their way, and in this case, he was more than happy to oblige. The matchmaker (*schadchan*) had done him proud. Rosa lived with her mother not far away in Suwałki. Her father had died some years before. Hirsch knew that he would be taking on quite a responsibility but he was ready for that. Rosa's mother was a traditional Litvak, Jewish widow: small and round, her head covered with a scarf that pulled her hair back from her strong, lined face. She looked much older than her years, but each wrinkle, each bold crease, had been made by hard experience; they told any onlooker that here was a woman who coped. She wore a plain grey pinny wrapped around her wide girth, with a handy front pocket usually bulging with all those things it was easy to mislay. The apron covered a simple dress which matched perfectly her flat, sturdy shoes. She stood four-square on any land and held her own, whatever the situation. She was, without doubt, a force to reckoned with. It was a good job: to be a widow with a child was no easy task or life. Fortunately, it was hard (at least at this point) to see in Rosa any likeness to her mother. Perhaps he wasn't looking straight, and to be honest, he knew that Rosa had not faced any of the challenges that her mother had taken on her broad shoulders. Not that he didn't admire the old lady, or appreciate the fact that she liked him and welcomed him as head of a new family, but if he was cruelly candid, she didn't stir the loins. Unlike Rosa, whose presence he (literally) felt and struggled to hide. Sylph-like, Rosa looked so much more vulnerable. She was a slight, little thing with dark, long hair, though always modest and well-hidden with a scarf. He loved her thin lips, which quivered a little when she was nervous or angry. And her dark Jewish eyes that glistened, bright and alert. I suppose you could say that once the matchmaker had done his work, they fell in love, enough anyway to begin with to find a base for a family life. She knew how to keep a home, she cooked well, given what little there was to cook with, and they went with all the family to the synagogue. And she knew how to deal with the stiffness in his loins!

The wedding was a modest affair by any standards. The mother-in-law (*Di Shviger*) made enough golden chicken soup to feed the neighbourhood, the most wonderful soggy dumplings and then *flodni* (layered pastry with apples, walnuts, currants and poppy seeds) to die for. It was a rare change from the daily *borscht*; how he tired of mashed potato and beet. What Rosa's mother lacked in the beauty department she certainly made up for in creating food for the hungry belly. With his sturdy practical mother-in-law and his thin-lipped, flower-like wife, life seemed good, at least for a now. His father and mother were proud of their son and took to the Schimanskis, especially the dainty Rosa.

The Rudamina synagogue was little more than a room with

chairs, a simple tabernacle for their precious purple velvet wrapped scrolls at the east end, and a *bimah* at the centre. As they stood under the marriage canopy (*chuppah*), he watched, with his eyes lowered, as Rosa circled him seven times, one for each time Joshua circled the great walls of Jericho, and he knew his own walls had fallen too. He was entranced by her simple grace and beauty. When the Reb gave him the glass to break, he felt not just the joy of the day; the sound of the glass crashing under his feet reminded him that there would be things to mourn, too. The sound pierced his happiness, like a lightning bolt bursting through the gathering dark clouds of an ominous future. He shook himself down. Now he had responsibilities, now he had a beautiful wife and a family to lead. He turned his face to the future with some resilience, and at least a small dollop of fear, topped with hope.

Home was two simple rooms in Rudamina – not counting the outside latrine shared by more than one of the slanted wooden shacks that filled street. For now, at least they had a marital bed, in a room of their own. They shared the kitchen with *Di Shviger* and the others, but there was a small room for them, too, with an old sofa covered in a crocheted blanket, a rickety table with an embroidered cloth, and some simple, cheap chairs. It wasn't paradise but it was a life. He had his place, his people, his way. Sadly, and slowly, things changed, and not for the better. It started with rumours, but the dark clouds became a reality, not an omen, and they were more menacing than they had imagined.

4

The mystery that is Joe Daniels

Joe (a diminutive of Joseph) – 'God will add'

No informal, slapdash nickname here.

Instead, a hidden dream, a dare to wear a coat of many colours.

A tentative step to grow different, to add a new dimension.

Yet in the end half-hearted, limp, almost shy.

All disguised in half a name.

Never to be fully found.

Geoff had heard about Joe Daniels long ago, perhaps when he was knee high to a grasshopper, but it took until much later in life for his curiosity to intensify. It was on his parents' wedding day that this name was revealed – to his father, at least. Hal was just seventeen and about to get married to his young, and pregnant, bride. Vee was sixteen and somewhat bewildered, and it wasn't just her hormones in overload. She had braved the scenes at home when her secret pregnancy was finally let out of the bag. She was relieved when she and Hal decided to get married. Now she faced the move into his house on Heywood Street with not a little trepidation. His mother, Mary Ellen, had a reputation, and one that she lived up to. Vee was terrified of her and what the future might bring. But right now, it was the wedding ceremony that occupied her thoughts. There was no time or money or enthusiasm for a posh do. She had managed to scrape enough money to get a new suit: grey with ruby-red trimmings. After the ceremony they would go to the pictures. Perhaps to see *The Curse of the Cat People*, starring Simone Simon and Kent Smith, which was hardly romantic and a film that frightened Vee well into her 50s, or then again maybe this time they would see *Cover Girl* (probably Vee's choice), with Rita Hayworth and Gene Kelly. Though, looking back, this was hardly a film for Hal, but perhaps a little romance on the day wouldn't hurt. The Gaumont was like a second home to them both; they had their favourite seats on the back row.

Vee arrived for the marriage at St Margaret's Church in good time. She knew the church from school days and on the odd occasion she had attended Sunday School when she was little. It was well known locally, easily spotted by its Victorian spire on the junction of Whalley Road and Rufford Street. She vaguely knew the vicar from school days, and had met him with Hal to prepare for the wedding.

When she arrived, she knew that something was not right. Hal was in the vestry with the vicar; they were deep in some kind of troubling conversation. Hal was just about holding himself together but she could see his anger, she noted his red neck, its vein throbbing and then his clenched fists by his side. The vicar, a wet rag at the best of times, was shaking, nervously looking around, as if expecting an unwanted guest. Hal took Vee's hand and said, 'Let's just get this over with, Vee!' Not quite the romantic affair of her childhood dreams. 'Just go along with things and I'll explain later,' he said, adding to the troubling mystery that was slowly opening itself to her. She trusted Hal, which proved to be a good job.

Later, he explained that the vicar had told him that his birth certificate, the one Mary Ellen (his mother) said she would give to the vicar herself because she was having trouble finding it, revealed that Hal was in fact really called Maurice, and his dad was not Pa (aka Walter Miller) with whom he had grown up but someone called Joe Daniels! Mary Ellen couldn't keep the secret any longer but despite Hal's questioning, she would tell him nothing else. From the day of his marriage to the day of his death, he didn't know who his father was. Her lips were sealed, she declared, and she meant it. For Hal, this became a life-long disturbing mystery. A code that couldn't be cracked. Mary Ellen refused to help and yet she was the one who could so easily have offered the solution. It became a riddle that niggled and ate him away at him, and a riddle he passed on to his children.

That sounds rather more dramatic than it really was. For Geoff, it became a fascinating, but not a disturbing mystery. There were a few hints that came Hal's way, loaded with intrigue. It appeared that Mary Ellen had been married before she became Mrs Walter Miller. Her first husband called himself Joe Daniels but Joe became impossible to trace. If he had lived, it was impossible to find his birth registration, and there was no death recorded in the data Geoff consulted. Of course, there are (and were) plenty of Joe Daniels in the Manchester region but they didn't seem to fit the bill, either in dates or details. It seemed like this Joe Daniels appeared from nowhere and just as easily slipped away into oblivion. Hal had one other memory: being snatched by a man in black when he was a small child and a policeman returning him home. Was that Joe? Hal tried on many occasions to find out more, but without success. It bothered him, but he was not obsessed. His unfulfilled search was part of his legacy to his children. Hal's curiosity was never resolved, nor did it diminish.

Geoff became intrigued about his roots. Now, in the first wind of his retirement, Geoff fantasied about his mysterious grandad Joe. A bigamist? A spy? He could invent many exciting possibilities. In the end what he discovered took him hundreds of miles (virtually, if not physically), and forced him into new places and cultures that bore little resemblance to his present home. Yet in his early attempts, the secret would not give itself up.

5

Simchat Torah –

an ending and a beginning

Simchat – Hebrew celebration

Joy springs from the depths.
It is music and laughter, food and dancing.
It can signal the conclusion
or it is there at the start.
It shouts hope, even in the night.
New possibilities
for everything lie ahead.
Don't look back.

The 13th March 1881 was not a particularly significant date in the mind of Hirsch Karavitch. It should have been! Not that knowing what had happened on that day would have changed much, but it might have provided a possible explanation. Happenings on the national (or international) stage often trigger local events. However, things become a thousand times more toxic when such events collude with local rumour, local prejudice, local fear, local thuggery.

The assassination of Tsar Alexander II sent shockwaves throughout the Pale. The rumours that followed in its wake had an equally vicious impact. Like all rumours, they worked with a grain of truth to manipulate, use and abuse. The government blamed the assassination on 'foreign influences', a code word for 'Jews'. Two of the conspirators were said to be Jewish, though that was never verified. The press had a field day, and fanned the flames of anti-Semitism. Tsar Alexander II, and his son Tsar Alexander III, had no love of Jews to begin with, and this only exacerbated their hatred.

The Pale had, in a strange way, both restricted the Jewish community and at the same time provided a degree of freedom, as long as they stayed within its borders. Kovno became a prosperous centre and its Jewish community had shared in the prosperity. Indeed, they had made a significant contribution to it. A thriving Jewish culture had developed: an internationally renowned *Yeshiva* (a Jewish University), a theatre and music hall, as well as vibrant commercial activity. That said, it wasn't prosperous for everyone and a lot of the poorer Jews, those like Hirsch and Rosa, only survived through wider family support and the ever-present Jewish welfare charities. Welfare charities fortunately proliferated, as did associations of various kinds, not least some political movements such as the developing Bund.

Tsar Alexander III increased restrictions for Jews through the so-called May Laws. These limited travel and habitation, and disenfranchised Jews from political office and participating in elections. Of course, the Laws meant more tax was demanded, too. More crucially, it fed into an already existing hatred and relentless scapegoating of Jews: 'They steal our jobs, they cheat us out of our money, they take over our towns!' was the bigot's cry. Like a low-lying, creeping smog, the vibrant Jewish community became defensive, nervous, on edge. Things were changing, and not for the better. Hirsch's fears started to come true.

It started slowly and, in the scale of things, quite mildly. They arrived early for work one day. The shop was still locked and bolted, the shutters closed. But on the very same shutters were daubed the words 'Dirty Jews!'. Offensive, hurtful even, but more importantly a signal that the temperature was rising. A morning had to be spent cleaning the paint before they could settle down to tailoring for the day. A few days went by and things seemed eerily calm, everyone watching and waiting, watching and waiting, which only raised the temperature higher. It wasn't just the Karavitch tailor's shop: other shops, businesses and some (hopefully random) houses suffered the same fate. There was talk of threats, of small crowds of youths loitering on street corners with some kind of intent. Nothing happened; things were ominously quiet.

A week or so later, maybe less, Rosa told him that one of the other women had been approached by a group of lads who shouted the usual things at her. She was alone and no one was around. She ran, frightened, until she found a house she recognised and sought safety. Hirsch cautioned Rosa not to take too much notice of gossip but to be careful. He thought it may be a bit of hysterics but he was still a little worried. Then it became personal. He was walking home, a little earlier than usual, when he heard a scream. He turned the corner to see Rosa crying on the pavement and a group of lads running away. Without thinking, he gave chase then ran back to Rosa. She wasn't greatly hurt but very shaken. They had stolen her shopping bag. There were a few such attacks that day and though the police were polite, they showed little serious interest. Later that night, a group of *goy* thugs went on the rampage in the neighbourhood, smashing the windows of the shops and some houses, and shouting anti-Jewish slogans. The police were nowhere to be seen, indeed they were definitely absent.

Things were getting worse by the minute and the community was frightened and angry; not a good combination. It was that night that a frightened and shaking Rosa lost their first child. They had stolen much more than the shopping. The little household was devastated. This was now very personal. Once the bleeding started, Hirsch called Dr Cohen but it was all too late. Rosa now needed rest, good wholesome food and lots of comfort. Comfort which Hirsch felt totally inadequate to give. Like a fish riding a bike, he was out of his depth. He watched her thin, quivering lips, her quiet soul crying, and his own heart bleeding, aching, pierced for her. He should have known, should have done more, should have protected this fragile flower, bowed and drooping before him. Fortunately, her mother was on hand to offer comfort and, of course, chicken soup.

The next day he arrived at the shop early. It was grim; a dark cloud coloured the already gloomy work room. They picked up their work for the day without much talk. Anxious colleagues with little to say to each other, but every look, every moment of silence spoke a thousand words. Isaac kept his head down, *too* down, thought Hirsch. He passed him a hot drink, a smile, an attempt to show some support. As he looked, he saw Isaac's glasses: there was a large crack in one lens and the other lens was shattered.

'Isaac, are you alright, cousin?' he asked.

'Of course.' He was curt in his reply. The quavering voice of a man feeling shame.

'The glasses – what happened?'

Isaac, head down, pleaded. 'Don't ask, please don't ask. They smashed them, they humiliated me, they destroyed me!'

'Who?' Hirsch gently questioned.

'I don't know, some thugs, some *goys*, a crowd of them.'

Tears filled his eyes as he continued to look down, hiding his face, not daring to meet his eyes. He was broken. You could smell the fear.

That night, Hirsch joined a meeting of other men from the

neighbourhood at the synagogue. News was that theirs wasn't the only place to see a rise in violence against the Jewish communities. It was widespread in Kovno, in Suwałki, and no doubt in Vilnius itself, not to mention the surrounding towns, and likely deeper into the Pale. A brigade to protect the neighbourhood was easily formed. People were brave in the idea, less so in the reality. Still enough supported the regular patrols. Hirsch did his bit, but faced his fight or flight, a strong, powerful mechanism that penetrated his thoughts, his dreams, his breathing. Each and every time, he imagined Isaac with his smashed spectacles, every moment he recalled his wife quaking with fear, her wide eyes and quivering lips. Was this the time to go? Time to leave it all behind? Everything he had always known. Was somewhere else safer? Now he had responsibilities. Now people depended upon him. Now it wasn't just the present, but his whole future that dominated his every breath.

With a heavy heart, he dragged his feet to the synagogue to take his turn on the patrol. First, he checked that the house was closed and that he had barred the shutters and locked the doors. There was a good crowd waiting in the synagogue foyer, though not a happy one. No one liked this task but there was at least some camaraderie. They walked the neighbourhood together in small groups; tramped the wood-paved walks along the sides of the slanted houses. It began to rain. It was cold and dark and you never knew what was around the corner. As he walked, he could feel the fear in his own body but also in the air, palpable like a menacing spectre. And as he walked, he could smell the poverty. Dirt everywhere, clinging to their shoes, mud on everything they touched. He was struck almost suddenly with a deep ache. Is this all I have, my only place, my only world, or is there something beyond the fears, beyond the dirt, beyond the drudgery? Things had seemed to calm down but they still lived on high alert. The situation could turn on the toss of a coin, the shout of a derisory comment that wasn't ignored, the chase of a group of thugs or the daubing of a wall.

In the workshop, they kept themselves busy; it was the only way to keep warm. Shabbat came and went, came and went, with its pulsing regularity. Sometimes they joined the whole Karavitch household, on others (though rarely), they stayed at home. They kept a kosher house. They welcomed the sabbath as Rosa, or his mother, lit candles, covering her eyes as she said the blessing. As the meal finished, he, or his father, would say the *Kiddush*. But they were not really very pious believers. The synagogue was the meeting place of their neighbourhood but Hirsch did little Talmudic study – well, not since his *Bar Mitzvah* days. The Karavitchs tried to fit in, they didn't follow any particular 'wind or fancy' as his dad called the different ideas and fashions that swooped through the community. Keep your head down and try not to be noticed, try to be part of the crowd.

Hirsch arrived early at the shop on the Sunday morning. The others dribbled in, the younger one quite bleary-eyed. There was no Isaac. Lunchtime came and went and still no Isaac.

'Is my cousin Isaac ill?' he asked Eli.

'Not really,' Chaim replied. 'He's gone, gone for good.'

'Gone where, Uncle Chaim?'

With a deep sigh, Chaim answered his question: 'He was humiliated, he couldn't take it anymore. I bought him a one-way ticket to freedom.'

'And where is freedom, Uncle, where is freedom? Tell me, please!'

In this case, freedom turned out to be Dublin of all places; a place where Jews were welcome, even prospered. A place that needed tailors, cutters and pressers. A few weeks passed and Abraham followed his brother, leaving just two of them to work the machines. But work was diminishing fast. They weren't the only ones to go. Throughout the *shtetel*, gaps appeared, sometimes whole families left, usually under the cover of darkness. Silently, or at least quietly, people left for the paradise that was USA or Dublin in Ireland or South Africa. Dublin became an extension of Rudamina, a foreign embassy if you would. A Litvak oasis.

Hirsch talked to his father, and then to Rose. Was this the time for a Karavitch move, time to chase a dream? Or was it chasing the end of a rainbow, an Irish rainbow? He spoke no English, in truth he had no idea where Dublin was. How would he get there? Who would he take with him? Could they find somewhere to live in a foreign country, would there be work, food, a life there? No one could answer yes or no to these and so many other questions that troubled him. There were no certainties. They could follow the others, but they might risk more than they could gain. There again, they could stay and, in doing so, might lose everything. Staying in Rudamina might throw away a chance for all of them to have a new life. A free life, not one filled with fear, dirt, poverty and drudgery.

October came, and the synagogue and the neighbourhood prepared for *Simchat Torah*. A joyous time of merrymaking, eating, drinking and having fun that marked the end of the year's cycle of reading Torah and the beginning of a new one. A season of endings and beginnings, if you will. A torchlight procession led by the children waving flags marched to the synagogue. Hirsch watched his mother-in-law and Rosa bend to kiss the velvet of the Holy Scrolls as they were processed throughout the tiny synagogue. And as they began their sevenfold dance, carrying the scrolls around the *Bimah*, he remembered the day of his marriage, when in a similar circling, the walls around him tumbled down. Once, twice they jostled around to joyous singing and dancing. He glimpsed his sylph-like, vulnerable Rosa bend to bestow her kiss, her delicate lips touching the velvet, heavy-brocaded cover just as they had so often. Then he brushed his lips to the scrolls with a distant reverence and the walls came crashing down yet again. The circles, and the dancing, became louder, more frenzied. *Oh Joshua, Oh Jericho, Oh my Rosa!* In a moment he knew beyond doubt it was a time for an ending, a time for a new beginning, a time to create a life beyond the Pale.

6

What to do with three bottles of vodka

Vodka – Slavic for 'dear little water'

Let's raise a toast to vodka,
A sting slurring slurp for freedom.
The best kind of shot that warms the stomach
and changes the landscape,
and dumbs the pain.
It is worth raising the glass and burning the toast:
Here's to a new world.

Intention, even decision making, is easy; acting it out is quite another thing. After a short-lived exhilaration, glimpsing *Goldene Medina* (the USA), Hirsch came back into the real-time world of Rudamina, Russia, with a bit more than a bump. Whatever he did now he had to do it with care, not on impulse; step by step, not running too fast into trouble. He talked again with Rosa. Without her he couldn't even think any more about it. He had her family, as well as his own, to think about. The family gathered, a sombre gathering, but an essential one. Nathan, the father and head of the household, had called them together. He oversaw them in a gentle and wise manner. Never pushing too far, often opening up questions rather than giving orders, always encouragingly supportive. He knew about Hirsch wanting to leave but he also knew that Woolf had similar ideas. The family was disintegrating around him, but he also recognised that any future for his children did not lie in Rudamina. However, it was complicated. Woolf and Dora were older, they had no direct dependants. Dora's mother and sister were heathy and well able to travel later on their own. Perhaps Woolf should go first. Next, they needed to see how to get papers, passports, shipping tickets, addresses to arrive at, before they even began to count the cost. Nathan would stay in Rudamina with Golda; like Rosa's mother, she would struggle with such a hard journey. Maybe later they would join them when they were settled in foreign lands. So, a family plan began to emerge. Above all, this had to be done quietly, without any fuss, otherwise they would be stopped. Nathan would ask his brother for some advice, how it went for his lads. He would have to ask him about money too. Not easy for Nathan as his brother was always too ready to play the older, wiser brother.

Woolf and Hirsch consulted, in general terms, some of their peers. It was already the talk of the town. There were people who would help, agents who knew the ropes, who had contacts with authorities and shipping lines, but the difficulty was finding the ones you could trust and, of course, afford. Word on the street was that if you timed it right, and went on the best routes, the guards turned a blind eye and let you through. There were horror stories, too. People being left in strange foreign places with no shelter or food. Guards demanding excruciating back-handers just to let you pass and sometimes great confusion when you arrived. Nathan heard his brother recount similar tales. His lads were now firmly ensconced in Dublin. Reputedly the 'fairest city in the world' but Chaim was prone to stressing the good bits and gliding over the horror points. Apparently, there was a growing Jewish community in Dublin and nearly all of them were Litvaks.

'Home from home,' Chaim said, 'except no pogroms. Yes, it rains a lot but it's green, it has a fine university and there are jobs. Jobs for tailors, too.'

Both lads were doing well, he boasted as ever, and soon they would start their own shop, much bigger than the one they left behind. Of course, he admitted, they'd never intended to go to Dublin. They really wanted to go to *Goldene Medina*. Once they had saved enough, they probably would move on. But for now, life was good, they were successful.

'You should encourage your lads to do the same,' he advised. 'Make something of themselves. Make you proud.'

Nathan knew his brother; he was prone to exaggeration, especially about his lads. He had always been like that. His wife was the prettiest, his in-laws the wealthiest, his lads the most intelligent. And, of course, he had a thriving tailoring empire on the corner of Bolshaya Street and Schneider Street. Something he seemed to have to remind Nathan of every time they met. But Nathan allowed him his bit of grandiose musing; this was nothing new. He knew the shop, he knew Dora, he knew the lads, he had heard it all before many times. But he was his brother after all. Nathan was already proud of his own good lads without lessons from Chaim. But he couldn't be so cruel as to burst Chaim's bubble. Chaim was quite capable of doing that for himself.

'How come this place you call Dublin? How come there?' Nathan gently inquired. 'Is there family there or some contacts? Is that why they went there first rather than straight to *Goldene Medina*?'

'It's a long story, sit down brother, and we will share a vodka or two.' Chaim was wanting to talk. He was missing his lads.

They sat by the fire while Dora worked in the kitchen behind them. Chaim started to tell his tale and the warmth, as well the vodkas, helped loosen his lips.

'Thank G-d,' he explained, 'they have found good support in Dublin. There are people from Suwałki and Kovno there and the Jewish Relief Society helped them when they arrived. A few hundred Jews live there and most are from Kovno and the surrounding *shtetls*. But the story isn't all good. In truth, they arrived there by mistake. They went via Hamburg and the journey was horrendous, taking the best part of five days. When they arrived in a port called Hull, in the north of England, they thought it was the USA, though they were shocked that it was smaller than they'd expected. The Jewish Relief Society explained it was the UK and helped them get a train to Liverpool from where they were told they could get another boat straight to *Goldene Medina*. They did manage to board another boat, it cost them everything they had for the tickets, but they were confused at the signs. When they arrived and came ashore they found that it was Dublin! There were Litvaks there who helped them find a hostel to stay in and they decided that for now it was best to stay there. Then they found rooms with an old Jewish woman who had helped them. So, there they are in Dublin, but safe, thank G-d. The synagogue there is full of people from Suwałki and Kovno, even a family from Rudamina. So now we have an Irish tailor in the family, living in Little Jerusalem, Dublin. G-d bless them.'

Nathan went home, warmed by the vodka and contemplating the information he had gleaned. It would be a tough time if his lads followed; it would break Golda's heart and not do much for his own, but he knew the best hope for the future was to help his lads leave. Perhaps when they had settled in Hull or Ireland or *Goldene Medina*, he and Golda could join them, G-d willing. But there was some work, and much preparation, to do first.

Tailors were not best paid in Russia even in the largest and most prestigious workshops, never mind in Rudamina. At Chaim's poor workshop, they got a pittance. The brothers did some homework only to find that buying shipping tickets, even in steerage, and getting hold of passports was a costly and volatile business. They estimated that they would need at least the equivalent of one annual wage for each couple to make the journey. Nathan asked around about local 'agents' who could undertake the travel arrangements. One friend at the synagogue recommended not travelling through Germany but rather to head north to Libau. The Wilson Shipping Company had recently joined with the Union Castle Line to create an easier, and cheaper, route to the UK and beyond. The Wilson Line was already the largest cargo shipping line in the world, taking goods from Libau – mainly wood – to the UK. They also carried some passengers in steerage; it was a quieter, more discreet route, at least for now.

So, the plan began to develop, to grow some flesh, so to speak. Woolf and Annie would go first, maybe Annie's sister Bessie and their mum might go with them but they would decide that later. For now, it was pooling their savings. Then applying for papers. As great a hurdle as that was, it was the easy bit, for sure.

Nathan contacted the local agent suggested by Chaim. He seemed to get good recommendations from others too, and his family could be trusted. So, the Karavitch plan was put into action. After much thought, they decided not to aim for the new world but to go straight to Dublin. After all, they had family contacts there, and they could move on later if they wanted. Woolf could settle and earn some money to send back for Hirsch. Hirsch and Rosa agreed to wait patiently. In retrospect, it proved a wise move.

The months went on, but now life was different for them all. Plans to move had reconfigured the chess board, so to speak. Now they harboured a secret, a strategic plan for the future. Each day was no longer just another day but different, another day towards the plan's fulfilment. Sorting out Woolf's arrangements was no easy task but they learnt a lot as they went along, and it was learning that would prove useful, even life-saving for Hirsch.

Getting the passports and tickets became the first significant hurdle to overcome. It was a minefield of obstacles and not a cheap task. Of course, it began at base with a set fee or charge, but that was just the start. Soon they would learn that nothing in this domain worked by simple, overt sets of fees. Finding the right official and the right bribe was the real art. Such skill was way beyond Woolf and his family's expertise or experience but there were those who would help – for another fee, of course. For both his sons' travels, Chaim had used an agent based in Suwałki. Chaim helped them contact the people smuggler (or emigration consultant or agent – take your pick) and begin the process. The time lapse between getting papers and actually leaving allowed them to muster funds on route.

Woolf remained convinced that they should aim to join his cousins in Dublin. It seemed not only a shorter route, but a less popular one. Perhaps it would be good not to travel with large crowds, especially if his mother-in-law and Annie's sister went with them. Also, the cousins' contacts in Dublin would hopefully help find accommodation and even some work. In reality, the papers and the fares would cost somewhere in the region of 400 roubles and then they would need some money to take with them for contingencies, and to pay for accommodation, food and emergencies. After that, when they arrived, no doubt they would have to rely on local relief societies, but Isaac and Abraham would be there to help.

By early autumn, they decided that they had saved enough to start the process, though as the time approached, they became more than a little apprehensive.

*

They had a farewell gathering at Nathan's on the night before they left. Nathan opened a bottle of vodka and they all had a tot, well, the men had more than a little, but they persuaded Annie, Rosa and even Imma to try a little, for courage, consolation and good wishes. They sang some of their favourite Litvak songs, they ate the famous chicken soup and they cried. They laughed too, but they knew that this might be the last time they would be together, certainly in Rudamina. In the end, Annie's mother and sister decided to follow later. So, it was just Woolf and Annie who boarded the 'agent's' cart when it collected them, in the cover of a dark and sleeping village. Two more gaps would appear the next morning in the community, and the family had only prayers and blessings left to give them and send them on their away. It would be many weeks before they heard any news. It was a long journey by cart and train to Libau, and the agent proved to be bossy, surly and somewhat threatening. Woolf clasped his papers close to his heart and his money closer. The agent explained to them that they would need to get a boarding pass each in exchange for the tickets. Woolf was unsure whom he could trust, so he trusted no one. Annie was frightened all of the time. She was wide-eyed, shaking, her lips trembling, and she grasped Woolf tightly around his arm. As they neared Libau, the final bit of the journey by cart, they stopped in a wood while the agent went to do business for them. There was perhaps a dozen of them. Cold, with no food left, they waited, shivering, scared of the strange darkness. They had no idea where they were or what would happen next. They waited quietly, silently. Bereft of trust, frightened, bewildered. At first, they waited patiently but soon more nervously, then fear took over. It began with a manic whispering, a whimpering that seemed to get louder and louder. Male voices tried to subdue it. 'Shut up, woman!' said one of the men to his wife. But the tone of his voice only revealed his own growing fear. The dark, glistening pupils of their eyes were visible, even in the night. They could not keep still, agitated, moving from one foot to another or tightly huddled to protect themselves from the cold of the night, their eyes darting in every direction. They were growing colder and hungrier by the minute, yet they did not leave the wood, they still waited. They had no other option. As the darkness enveloped them, it was the sound of the trees and the birds that made the woods feel menacing. Bats flew from side to side high above them, their shadows tracing the trees and making the sky feel full and dangerous. Woolf remembered a magnificent white owl that hovered above them, its huge wings spread out like a floating roof to a non-existent building. A predator hunting flesh or a wise old bird, a sign of protection? *This is crazy*, he thought. *We know woods, we have lived among them all our lives.* Yet that night, somehow, old forest friends became threatening, dark and dangerous unknown forces. Terrified, they stayed together in the dark and cradled their families tightly, unsure and hesitant about touching others. Those travelling alone, one or two young men, looked lost, forlorn scared.

With momentous relief, they heard the rumble of the agent's cart wheels and his loud whisper. You could sense the tension dissipate, drift away like a unified sigh. They had not been totally abandoned, at least not yet. People breathed out, their shaking slowly stopped, and only then did they feel the biting cold and the ache in their empty bellies. He had news, the agent told them. Not all bad, but not all good. He had bread and water enough for a little each. The harbour master was demanding more money to release the boarding permissions. They would have to pay a further 10 roubles each and hope that would be enough to satisfy him. The agent said he was one of the better masters, so they just needed to be patient and trust. What choice did they have now? Woolf quietly counted out the money, his resources diminishing by the minute. He began to yearn for the fireplace in Rudamina.

The port, when they arrived, was in chaos. As dawn was breaking, it was crowded and noisy, jostling stevedores moving heavy freight and desperate passengers manically following whoever offered them a lead. Cargo and people were hard to distinguish apart and on reflection it was to remain like that until they disembarked. However, with their agent shouting out orders, holding on to each other for dear life, they boarded the ship and scrambled to find a space to lie down. They felt like animals being transported for slaughter; they were treated like that too. A tiny open deck space was the only opportunity to find fresh air and even that was polluted with the smell of the diesel engines, and later on during the passage with the growing vomit and even worse the sewer drainage from the other decks.

Inside, it was dark, the smell of human sweat overpowering, and as the journey finally began, vomit splashed over the floors and benches, which remained uncleaned, fermenting and festering. They found a tiny berth against a wall to share, which at least had a curtain they could pull across to give them a little decency. It was their only space for sleeping, dressing and eating. The stench of the toilets was overpowering. The journey was insufferable and at times felt intolerable. But where could they go? They lurched up and down, up and down, with each swell. Sometimes they were thrown across the passages in the sway, often having to avoid furniture and luggage, pans and glasses that flew above their heads or landed on the deck. They counted four days and nights. As the violent motion continued to throw them side to side, their stomachs emptied with a shuddering regularity. If this was their journey to freedom, they certainly paid the price – and not just in roubles.

They arrived in a damp Hull. A sea fret masked the darkened landscape. The fuel burning smoke from the chimneys of the rows upon rows of houses added to the soot smell that coloured the grey mist. Fortunately, Abraham's graphic letters to his father had prepared them and they knew this was not *Goldene Medina*. They anticipated the next step but were thankful, eternally grateful even, for the Jewish Reception Agency's welcome. For food and a wash, and to feel they were in safe hands at last. They boarded the Northern Line train from Hull city and, because they were ultimately heading for Dublin, they were slightly aloof from the mass crowds trying to board the steamers that would cross the Atlantic. They dreaded being on board a ship again but it was a mercifully short crossing and they disembarked into another grey and damp city. Perhaps this was how freedom would have to look, at least for now. Their cousins met them and took them to the rooms they were renting in Little Jerusalem.

Soon Woolf and Annie were ensconced in Dublin's 'fair city'. They found work in a sweatshop, but at least it paid the bills, and they were able to save a little to go towards the next Litvak consignment of émigrés.

*

Back home in Rudamina, plans suffered a major hiccup. Ma Schimanski (*Di Shviger*), Rosa's mother, took ill. They didn't notice her struggling at first; she was too proud to show them. Her breathing was laboured and she looked tired. In a few weeks, she went from being a force of nature to a tired old lady, bed-bound, barely able to drink from her cup. Dr Cohen had no answer; all he offered was a solemn shake of his head. Rosa nursed her well, coaxing her to drink a little soup, take water, try a few vegetables. Golda helped, as did the neighbours, but it was clear she would not recover. Any thoughts of leaving were as far from their heads as *Goldene Medina* was from Suwałki. It was a painful time; she had been so good to them and Hirsch could honestly say he had grown to love her. When they were first married, she'd scared him a little, he didn't mind admitting. She was fearsome, solid, almost immoveable. But she treated him like a son, and in time, as the head of the family, all rolled into one. She respected him, fed him, cared for him and doted on Rosa. She would help Rosa wash and darn the clothes, sew the sheets and make pretty table decorations. He knew she loved him too. The occasional smile in his direction, the raising of the eyebrows when Rosa was angry with him, the way she came to him for advice on money and bills. She was his *Di Shviger* and now she had little time left on this earth. Rosa and he spoke with the Burial Society in the town and they gathered by her bedside, reciting prayers from the *Book of the Sick and Dying*. A monotone hum rung from her bedroom as she lay there. Rosa could only cry, and it was Golda who sat with her day and night. Her death came quickly and almost unexpectedly at the end. The news was brought fast to Hirsch at the sweatshop and, on hearing it, he let out a deep sigh and tore his shirt. The women from the Society washed her body and placed it in the shroud that had been lovingly prepared years before. The following day they gathered in the cemetery and lowered the simple wooden coffin into the grave. The rabbi joined them, with many more from the community, as they prayed and read psalms. Hirsch, the closest male relative, had the honour and the responsibility of reciting the *Kaddish*:

'Exalted and hallowed be God's great name...'

He chanted, his voice deep, solemn and heavy, like his heart that day. He watched Rosa, her slim, beautiful lips gently trembling and her brave face stubbornly and proudly holding back her ready tears. She had been a good mother, and a good mother-in-law, but now she slept in peace. The following days were a blur. They never left the house, which was constantly full of visitors. Family, neighbours, distinguished community elders, all came to pay respects. So, they began a whole year of mourning, a year without celebration, a year of the daily recital of *Kaddish*, a year when plans for fresh starts were not mentioned or progressed.

Rosa was remarkable. He watched her grow and grow, mature and take on her new role. Her mother had prepared her for this, and she would have been proud to see Rosa move into it with grace and dignity. It was a sombre year and they missed the old lady. His own mother gently embraced Rosa, leaving her enough space to find her own way, but being close enough to support. They had time to save up hard-earnt roubles, and they never wavered in their decision to move; the idea never left them. In fact, if anything they were now even more committed to leaving the Pale and finding a new future. After a time, they had long-awaited news from Woolf and Annie. They understood that news would be at best somewhat spasmodic but in time it got through. Apparently, in no time Woolf had left Dublin and followed available work to another Irish city, called Belfast. It was a more industrial city with more jobs for tailors. In Belfast, Annie had her first child, a boy they proudly called Abraham. So, the family grew. Golda and Nathan itched, ached even, to see their grandchild but had to make do with knowing Annie and the child were safe. The situation in Suwałki thank G-d did not get much worse, but the atmosphere remained tense. It was as if they lived on permanent high alert. Occasionally, violence broke out and the men had to start their nightly rounds until it settled again. Close by, in Kovno, new trends caught people's imagination; perhaps they were shallow fashions, only time would tell. Many would drift into the mist but some would stick. The Bund, a more aggressive group fighting for Jewish rights, began its secret and volatile work, while others became fixated on Zion and hankered after making *allyah*, yet others set their faces against such Zionism and for a growing group more non-religious philosophies became popular in the cities. Most of this passed the Karavitches by; heads down and fingers on the scissors, they continued to keep the old customs. They were certainly not highly religious but stubbornly traditional. Rudamina remained, on the whole, sleepy, and thankfully there was enough work to feed themselves.

Soon another year had passed and they prepared for *Simchat Torah*. Again, they followed the parade of the scrolls, and again Hirsch remembered the promise he had made to himself about leaving the Pale.

Once the *avelut* year of mourning was completed, they began to plan more earnestly. Before they had made any arrangements, they received another letter from Woolf. He, Annie and Abraham had moved again, this time to a town called Manchester on the British mainland. It was in the North of England, not far from the port of Liverpool. Woolf said it was the best town for getting a tailoring job. In fact, it was the tailoring capital of Britain, he told them. Like the other cities, Hull, Dublin and Belfast, it was grey and damp, and it never stopped raining but it was also a city of innovation. He described the weaving machines powered by steam. The huge mills and the growing factories produced clothes in new and fast ways. Woolf explained that every piece of clothing to be made was broken down into separate tasks – cutting and hemming; buttons and button holes; lapels and pockets and so on. Tailors worked on a production line, performing just one of the tasks and passing the garment on to the next person who did their job. The garment was no longer made by one person but many. It was hard work, and boring, but fast, and it was better paid. There were still a few small tailor shops making bespoke garments and some people were beginning to work from home. 'This the future,' he wrote. 'Come to Manchester, come and join me here. We will build a new life. A Karavitch Empire.'

Not long after *Simchat Torah* in the year 5647-5648 (1887ce.), they calculated that they had enough money to begin the process. They contacted the agent in Suwałki and applied for the first set of papers. They waited and waited and, hearing nothing, thought that something was wrong. The agent explained his contacts in government had changed. There was talk of conscription for young Jewish males, which had increased applications for passports and the scrutiny of papers. They would have to wait for the right moment and as usual he needed more money for bribes. The little reserve which they had from Rosa's mother's savings, which they had wanted to keep aside for their first child, now, with a heavy heart, had to be handed over to the agent. Well, at least some of it. Suddenly, it seemed all rushed through and the agent gave them a date and a time. They made the final preparations, with apprehension and some fear but also excitement. Early in the day, Rosa had visited her mother's grave to say a last *Kaddish* there, to lay a stone and tell her mother of their plans. She needed her mother's approval, desperately. She arrived back calm and resolved. Mrs Schimanski ad done her motherly business from beyond the grave. That night they met again at Hirsch's parents to eat and sing, and to say goodbye. It was a depleted gathering compared to the last leaving they shared. But they remembered those not physically with them this time, and remembered them with love and gratitude. Nathan placed three bottles of vodka on the table. One they opened and tipped into their small glasses. They shared a toast to Mrs Schimanski, and they shared a blessing toast for the future. Their bellies were warmed by the alcohol, settled a little from the nerves that were beginning to rumble deep in their guts. Hirsch reflected that it was like a real-time Passover, except not 'next year in Jerusalem' but 'next year in

Manchester', wherever that was! To be honest, it did not have quite the same poetic feel but, in both cases, it meant the leaving of home and the finding of a new one. Both expressed hope for a better time. The second bottle Nathan put in a bag and gave it to Hirsch. 'Save this one,' he said. 'An emergency supply if you will. You may need it. If it survives the journey, give it to Woolf.'

There was a knocking at the door. They let the agent in. He was grumpy, curt, not someone to meet in a dark alley, and always in a furtive hurry. Now they must trust him with their lives. Nathan spoke with him and handed him a bag with the third bottle of vodka. 'A little something to warm you up, my friend,' he smiled. The agent grunted a miserable reply but accepted the gift. He was used to accepting gifts.

They boarded the primitive, rumbling cart with tears in their eyes and a great deal of apprehension in their bellies. 'Keep in touch,' Golda said amid her tears. 'Please keep in touch, my little ones.' Then she turned and went into the house; she could not bear to see them leave. She didn't want their last vision of her as a sad old lady, crying. The driver cracked his whip and the cart moved off. Hirsch held Rosa's hand tightly and she placed her head on his shoulder. She was shaking, and he was doing all he could to hold his nerve. Other passengers were picked up in the cover of the dark. No one spoke, but there was a gentle, haunting murmuring, deep sighs, all of which added to the grim, palpably scary, menacing trek that lay ahead. The journey was interminably long, they were cold and uncomfortable, but still people hid themselves from each other, leaning into the dark night. Hirsch looked up to the sky, black but punctured with glistening stars. He pointed upwards and turned to Rosa.

'See – your mother is looking over us!' he exclaimed, hoping against hope that she was.

The journey was almost exactly as Woolf had described, so Rosa and he were not as perturbed when they were left in the dark, dampness of the wood while the agent went to negotiate the boarding passes. Just like Woolf had warned them, he returned to ask for more money to bribe the harbourmaster. Hirsch was expecting it, though this time it was 15 roubles, rather than the 10 that Woolf had to pay. Interest, no doubt. Like a repeat film show, they were given a little bread and milk and their orders to get on the cart. Then with another sudden, loud crack of a whip, the cart left for the port.

It was there that things went differently, there at the bustling port that Woolf and Annie's experience parted from their own. They were hustled into a shed where the harbourmaster was distributing the passes. He was tall, intimidating, a large purple bulbous nose in the centre of his lined face, his hair swept back but unable to cover his large ears. He stood tall over everyone and it was hard to avoid his tiny piercing eyes. He held a large bundle of boarding passes. Waving them on high out of their reach, but almost allowing the grasping hands to touch them. And he was reluctant to part with them. Hirsch watched as people handed over belongings, cash, anything they were asked for, before they were passed the precious boarding card. As Hirsch and Rosa approached the desk, Hirsch breathed deeply; he felt tense, unsure this was going to go well. The harbourmaster asked to check their baggage and quickly he spied the bottle of vodka.

'Oh, my friend, this is just what we all need on a cold, busy night!' he laughed. 'I'll get some glasses. Come, share a tot with us?'

Hirsch did not know which way to turn or what to say, but the harbourmaster was not looking for a response. He called a few of his colleagues and they poured some of the vodka into shot glasses, including one for Hirsch. He raised his glass.

'To the future! It's good stuff!' he guffawed. 'Very good stuff, my friend. It warms the bits that other drinks will never reach!' he continued, laughing. His colleagues laughed with him. 'Drink up, my man, enjoy.'

Hirsch was completely dumbstruck but did as he was ordered. The harbourmaster waved two passes under Hirsch's nose.

'Here, my lad,' he said. 'Take these!' and he offered him the tickets. But at the very last minute, he held on to one of them. He looked directly at Hirsch.

'Have you any more vodka? We get very cold here!'

Hirsch quickly replied. 'I'm sorry, Sir, I just had the one bottle.'

'Well, that is a shame. Mr Karavitch, isn't it?' he said, looking at the papers. 'I'm afraid one half-drunk bottle will only provide one ticket.'

'Sir, do I need to give you some money, please?' Hirsch pleaded.

'Well, that would be bribery,' the harbourmaster said, turning to his colleague. 'We can't have that, can we, Vladimir? Now a gift, a gift that would keep us warm on a cold night, that would be different.'

He turned his red face, his neck with its throbbing purple veins, towards Rosa.

'A pretty wife you have there, Karavitch. I bet she keeps you warm on a cold night like tonight, my friend. Perhaps we could come to some special arrangement.' He waved the second pass under Hirsch's nose and smiled. 'Unless of course you could find another bottle of the fire-water.'

Hirsch was devastated, trapped. He felt weak at the knees as his arm went immediately around Rosa's trembling waist.

'We have to leave,' he whispered to Rosa in Yiddish. 'Quickly, we must go home.'

From behind him, there was a kerfuffle; the grumpy agent was heading their way.

'What is the matter here?' he asked the harbourmaster. Without waiting for a reply, the surly agent continued. 'My friend here forgot this; maybe that is what is holding up the queue.'

He handed Hirsch the bottle of vodka in a bag, the one his father had given him at the door.

'No doubt he has been looking for it. It was meant for you. A little gift on a freezing Libau night.'

The harbourmaster looked directly into Hirsch's eyes.

'Well, isn't that kind, isn't that just so kind? Look, Vladimir, Hirsch here has found another bottle of vodka to warm the cockles. I think we should give him, and his pretty little wife, their boarding passes right away. Don't you agree?'

He handed the second pass to Hirsch and the agent hustled both of them towards the ship quickly.

'Go well, *shalom chaverim!*' he said and the last they saw of him was a weak smile revealing his broken yellowing teeth, and perhaps a wink. Well, it looked like a wink but Hirsch couldn't be sure.

They boarded the ship in a kind of blur; they could not explain what had just happened. His father's blessing and his father's vodka, maybe? His mother-in-law looking down upon them perhaps? A glimpse of kindness from a surly agent, most likely. No need to analyse, he chided himself, just be grateful. The ship journey was everything Woolf had warned them of, and more. Vomit everywhere, the overpowering smell of human sweat and cramped quarters, *very* cramped quarters. They needed air, they needed food and water. It was hell but their narrow escape from the port had raised their adrenalin levels, and now they were just desperate to reach a new land and start a new life. To be safe, to be with family.

The journey to Hull seemed to last a life-time and beyond. Hirsch trusted no one because now they had no agent to protect them, even though the agent's protection was a surprise, a pleasant one, true. He kept Rosa close, they spoke to no one, they looked no one in the eye.

Four days and nights they counted, then the ship shuddered into the port. People became quiet as the ship bunched against the quayside. The only noise was from the crew, shouting orders and instructions to each other. They had no idea where they were but they had landed, so to speak. Just as Woolf had warned, they were welcomed by a green fog, rain and ice-cold air. But they were on land and it was air, not sweat or the smell of vile vomit.

The Jewish Relief Society met them with welcome food and a place to wash in fresh water. They were helped on to the train for Manchester. He prepared himself with some roubles rolled into bundles, expecting everyone to demand bribes. He didn't want to be fumbling for money. He was determined to be ready this time. Nothing bad happened, the Relief Society put everything in place. Washed, fed, relieved, they even had a proper seat – a bench, but a seat nevertheless. It all happened so quickly, so efficiently, and he was daring himself to relax a little. A few hours later, the rain welcomed them to Manchester. They got off the train to begin a new life. Hirsch had decided that he would begin this new life with a new name, they would both have new names: Harris and Rose. New names, new home, new jobs, new lives. Forget *Goldene Medina*, it was Manchester that would be their golden city; grey, foggy, damp, industrial Manchester. Home.

*

Woolf and Annie met them, hugged them. They cried together, then laughed and eventually they drank a 'safe' tot of vodka and shared some chicken soup. What else!

7

This is not *Goldene Medina*, Harris

Goldene Medina n. The term used by Eastern European Jews to refer to the United States. A miraculous hope that ends in disappointment.

It should be the land of the free,

New York, but maybe also London, Hull or Manchester?

Dreams of golden streets give way to the stench of streaming sewers

Sunshine bends to grey clouds and damp rain.

Riches vanish in the smog of chimneys and crowded houses.

Jennies spin and machines whirl.

This is no Goldene Medina.

There is an old Jewish joke that goes something like this: 'What is the difference between a tailor and a doctor?' The answer: 'A generation!'

Perhaps that was the dream of Harris when Rose gave birth to each of their children, but in true Jewish style it was especially so for the boys. It was probably a dream Harris shared with every first-generation immigrant when they first held their offspring up to the sky or stared in their tiny eyes. Grateful for a safe birth, a crying baby and a wife tired, weak, but still alive. Somehow a new father wants for his child everything he did not have for himself, and most of all the love of friends and family. But when he thought about it, he wanted to add good health, safety... the list grew and grew. He held the boy in his strong olive arms, a tiny scrawny thing with a good head of hair just like his grandad. Harris played with his delicate, perfect, grasping fingers. They were long and thin, with the tiniest of nails, unbitten, unbroken. Were these tailor's hands, he mused, or the fingers of a concert pianist, a renowned fiddler or perhaps, just perhaps, a lawyer or doctor? Hirsch looked at his own hands, wracked with wrinkles, the scars of work. Knuckles, swollen and cracked, nails bitten down with worry, manual hands that were punished day in day out yet barely scratching a living, barely enough money for the bread that this little one would need. Maybe not a doctor, he mused, but anything better than this he hoped as he held his new born boy. He quietly prayed and whispered in the baby's ears: *'Yevarechecha Hashem ve'yishshmerecha.'* (May God bless you and protect you. May God make His face shine upon you and be gracious to you. May God turn His face towards you and grant you peace.)

He cradled the boy as he looked out into the dank street. Row upon row of the same stone houses; only the colour of the doors could tell them apart. 'Colour' was too fine a word, really far too fine, for those doors. Browns and greys, dark greens and blacks. It mattered little because like the bricks and the washing they were soon covered in soot and ash. Even the rain was dirty. Harris mused for a while with his little boy. 'I'm not sure how we got here, son. Where we left was dark and muddy, but there were fields and lakes too. Perhaps one day you will see Rudamina too.'

Back in that tiny village he once called home, on the night of *Simchat Torah,* he had dreamt of arriving in the glittering sunshine of *Goldene Medina.* Life there, he knew for sure, was smiles and food, meat every day. Clothes were light and bright. Streets were wide with trees, lots of trees, with deep greens and reds that glistened in the sun. But through the window all he saw now was smog, dank and murky green, with constant drizzle, wet, cobbled streets and soot-covered bricks. The air caught your throat and no one was spared a hacking cough. People trudged by in old dark clothes, mufflers to keep warm, and caps (they seemed to like flat caps), and heavy hobnail boots that they dragged along, scraping the pavement as they went by.

He smiled at the baby and at Rose. Dear Rose, who looked so pale, so weary, so tired.

'*Yismach avicha v'imecha v'tageil yolad'techa.*' (This is our day of joy. As it is said, little one, 'Your father and mother will be jubilant; the woman who bore you will exult.)

Of course, he *did* know how they had got here. He remembered every painful, treacherous step, every breath-stopping check of their papers, every snarling, grabbing official. He recalled with pain each palm crossed with silver and especially the bottles of fire water. Thank G-d for the grumpy agent. Thank G-d for the vodka! Perhaps!

But home is not a land or a specific town, rather it is made of children playing, of roaring fires and shelter from the cold. It is made of washing blowing dry on lines and food round the table, flickering candles lighting up the room. It is made with people you know and love. It is a place where you recognise faces, where you can discern smiles and snarls. A place where you are known, by your name.

*

In a short time, with the help of Woolf, they had found rooms to rent and a job to begin. In no time, they had met other Litvaks all seeking a new life in this strange land that they would now make theirs. He and Rose had never attended the synagogue so much as they did now, but they went more to speak Yiddish, to make friends, to find new networks and to offer their help to others, than to pray. However, by good chance, perhaps Y-H-W-H would shine his face on them too.

Their first real house was on Berkley Street, Salford, on the east side of the Irwell, behind Strangeways ironworks and the brewery. It was a two-up-two-down terrace, and for the first time they had their own outdoor toilet. They were at home on the street, with neighbours who had come from near to Kovno. Others from Russia, too, so, of course, almost a street full of Jews. Woolf and Annie lived nearby. You could smell the chicken soup and dumplings, especially on Shabbat. The cooking aroma was a blessed reprieve from the stench of the old river nearby, and the dust of the metal works that not only filled the air, but dirtied the washing no matter how much Rose tried to bleach it away. There was a United Congregation Synagogue nearby on Cheetham Hill Road which many of the neighbours attended. Rose made friends easily.

Woolf and Harris got jobs first as tailors' pressers at Lewis's Pleating Works. Then at Mr Joseph's Waterproofing further down Albert Street. During WWI, they both worked as coal carters in Bradford Road colliery but after the war they went back to tailoring and got work as machinists at Premier Garments (waterproofing) in Derby Street.

But the brothers were ambitious and entrepreneurial; they had been well trained by their father and were not ready to rest in Berkley Street or Strangeways. They got on well, shared dreams and plans aplenty. Both had a flair for selling and both had a good eye for material. Remnants, quality remnants, became their business. They started small, buying and dealing from their homes, even a market stall for a short while. Soon they were ready to take a bigger risk. They opened a small remnant shop and, while Woolf continued to work as a manager at Lewis' Pleating Works, Harris gave up his job at Premier Garments and took Woolf's oldest son with him to open up the shop. They aimed at local shoppers, head-scarfed, rotund, waddling 'wifies', making clothes for their families and selling to their neighbours. These women knew a good deal when they saw one. They drove a hard bargain; they were tough, discerning to say the least. Later, the brothers would spread their wings to supply bigger enterprises, but that was after they had made a name for themselves. Their advantage was their know-how. They were experts in material of all sorts, they could feel thread, understood weights, recognised good weave, loved quality. They knew what would sell, they could haggle for prices and they could rework and repackage small bails into useful buys for the smaller customer without much cash. They earned the trust of their regular customers, and in time were more and more respected by the salesmen in the nearby mills. Making good contacts was in their blood. Above all, they were honest and reliable. Material was sold at fair prices and bills were paid promptly.

Soon, they expanded. Woolf joined them, then one by one the rest of the family got involved. Kaye's Fent Store was born, a veritable Karavitch emporium, as they developed a bigger shop/warehouse on Moss Lane, near the Brook's Bar tram interchange. As Chaim would have said back home in Rudamina, 'A good spot to do business.'

More than anything in these early years, Rose produced children. She and Harris were blessed with a quiver full that would have impressed the Psalmist. Rose was a wonderful mother, she kept an ordered house, a warm home, and her daughters soon began to help. Ma Schimanski would have been proud of her daughter. The girls were Rose's compatriots in the kitchen; they cooked and giggled together. She adored her lads, too. Each was different, each demanded a different approach. She loved to make small drapes, covers and decorations out of wool and cloth. Throws for the furniture in contrasting colours of pink and red and blue, crocheted in circles or squares, with a pretty, brighter single colour to edge the sewn together pieces. Pristine linen table cloths with delicate patterns embroidered on each corner, reproduced on napkins. She liked to put flowers in the house, even though they didn't last long, peonies and freesia with their pungent smells, and, of course, roses. Pink ones were her favourite. She hummed tunes from back home as she worked, just like her mother used to. She was like her mother these days, except in her waist size which, in spite of the multiple child births, she kept reasonably trim. Harris liked to watch her as she concentrated over domestic tasks, her thin lips slightly trembling as she wound the wool or pushed the needle through, and through again. With her presence, the house was warm and peaceful, though brimming with life and energy. She was its queen, its beautiful gracious queen, and each Friday she gathered her brood around the table, lit the candles and welcomed Shabbat. *Simchat Torah* remained, for both of them, the favourite of the annual festivals, for it was on that day in 1886 that they had first decided to leave Rudamina for a new beginning, to find their *Goldene Medina*. Look where they landed! Harris loved her more and more as the weeks and years went by.

They never ventured far from home. 'Why, what for?' they would proclaim. They were settled, at peace. They did travel once, to the Lake District by steam train. It was a rare outing and the only time they allowed themselves the nostalgia of thinking back to Rudamina. Prompted by the intoxicating smell of fresh air, the green, green hills and the lakes, of course the lakes. For a fleeting moment they were back in Lazdijai, but they had few regrets when they remembered they were in England. They were just as pleased to get back to Moss Lane.

Rose knew the butcher and he would save her good cuts, and she was friends with the doctor's wife, whom she had met at the synagogue wives' group. At the little row of shops nearby, all her daily needs were easily met: groceries such as cheese, butter and bread and pastries when she hadn't time to make her own. The town centre wasn't too far away, easy to get to on the tramway, and there she could find shops like she had never seen back home. Shops stocked with every luxury you could imagine. Most of which she didn't need or desire.

Occasionally, very occasionally, they would walk in one of the parks. She liked Whitworth Park, but Alexandra Park was better. She would walk around the lake and watch the birds in the trees. To see a tiny robin feeding worms on the ground made her smile and she loved the colourful rhododendrons in spring.

Both Rose and Harris were thrilled when old Nathan travelled from Rudamina and came to live with them. Saddened at the death of Golda, how they wished that both *bubbes* could have seen their fine grandchildren. Nathan looked much older than his years, tired, a little stooped, his beard long and slightly unkempt. He missed his wife chastening him to cut it. Most of the time he simply sat with his pipe and tasted a nip of vodka now and again, smiling to himself, lost in his thoughts. He liked to visit the shop some days to see the material.

'Such choice,' he would say. 'Such choice you have.' He was proud of his sons.

8

Shy? Mary Ellen, *shy?!!!*

Mary (Heb. Miriam): Beloved, but also plump or rebellious one

She was no Madonna of Moss Side
No theotikus for the industrial slum.
Perhaps once a whiff of beauty but short-lived,
now she stood round
and firm, on the side of assertive living.
A mistress of manipulation with an Oscar for the faint.
No Queen of Heaven, but a determined sovereign of Heywood Street.

'Cottonopolis', or Manchester, in the late 18th century was once described as the global engine of the industrial revolution. The 'shock city' attracted attention from east, west, north and south. A golden city where gruff mill owners and industrialists became the self-made mega rich, and liked to tell you so, in straightforward, unflinching and extended rhetoric. A city of invention and innovation. A growing centre of culture with music provided by Carl Hallé no less, its own Literature and Philosophical Society, a public library, developing colleges and centres of learning. In no time it became the world centre of weaving and cloth making; the ship canal brought the raw materials, and the creation of expert machinery took spinning and weaving to new heights. Even the weather obliged, with generous amounts of dampening rain.

Yet there was an inevitable shadow to its glittering reputation. Factories demanded labour, and the cheaper the labour the greater the profit margins. But even cheap labour needs to be housed. Almost all of the thousands of workers lived in squalid, damp, wretched conditions. Effluence flowed faster than the Mersey down the streets of filthy terraces. Often there were only two privies to two hundred and fifty people. Cholera lurked in every back lane and ginnel. Perhaps it is no wonder that Manchester also attracted and gave birth to activists and radicals of all sorts, even the renowned Engels and Marx. Though to be fair, its radicalisation had taken place at least a century before; check out the infamous Peterloo Massacre.

But as Mrs Gaskell, Engels and Marx joined a plethora of observers documenting the scandalous poverty and wretchedness from their libraries, drawing rooms and desks, it was people, everyday humans, who lived in it. Some were born and bred Mancunians, others came from afar: Ireland and Eastern Europe the largest contributors. Thousands of people worked as wage-slaves, lived in poverty and destitution. They were poorly housed, poorly educated, unkempt and under-nourished. *Faiblesse* was bred in their genes, like a grit in the blood, visible in their downcast eyes and grey ragged clothes. For many, this was the reality of the great industrial revolution, this was the grinding life they had. It was a drudgery, devoid of hope. Some didn't take to it easily, and that Manchester radical spirit boiled over in more ways than social activism.

Take Mary Ellen Ellis, twenty and angry.

'You can stop that, right there! I've had enough of tongue and finger wagging to last a life time. So, I met a man and fell in love, what's strange about that? I didn't exactly take down all his details to see if they were acceptable to the general public. In case you didn't know, it doesn't work like that. Twenty bloody years cooped up in this dump, twenty years! "Do this, do that, wash this, clean that," like a bloody unpaid servant! Our Lou moaning and shrieking; Ma, no better than a wet rag; and him, him the ogre! No man will ever treat me like that, I can tell you. If I have learned anything it's that I'm going to live my own life, my own way and bugger the rest!'

Mary Ellen Ellis was not your average lass, at least on her street. Some called her feisty, others had different names, less polite ones. She was definitely a bolshie 'Manc', though hopefully they destroyed the mould that produced her. Though she wouldn't know, she certainly lived up to some of the suggested meanings of her name: the 'rebellious one' or the 'plump one'.

Mary Ellen was no pretty bombshell, no siren, but she had a certain air or flair. Round-faced with blonde wavy hair, she could make something of herself without too much effort, and she did. Though she was prone to a rounder body shape, she was able to keep it in check, most of the time. Small but not yet dumpy, with flesh in the right places. Her ample breasts, when young and pert, were perhaps her best advantage. When she could get it, she liked a bit of lip gloss and the odd bit of rouge, rubbed in, mind, not like dolls' cheeks, it had to be smoothed and spread. A pair of silk stockings occasionally rolled at the top to bring out a bit of the flapper in her. Heels just enough to firm up her calves and give her a bit of height. But on the whole, it was not her looks or her body that got her things: it was her style, her refusal to fit the norm, and especially her determination not to be dominated by anyone.

What was the attraction of Joe? He was different and he was

passive. God knows there was little else. He was just a bit exotic, foreign. Dark and tall, and perhaps not too bad on the eye. Actually, she quite liked his beard in some strange way. What she liked most was his dark piercing eyes and the way he looked at her. It was as if she were from another planet. I guess she might well have been a Martian to him. He was transfixed like a rabbit in the proverbial headlights. She swallowed up the devotion, greedily. He was the ticket she was looking for; well, that's what she thought then. 'A ticket to where? Who cares?' she thought. 'Just a ticket out. That would do – for now at least.'

She was hardly predatory but to be honest she was on the 'look out' for the exit sign. Perhaps that is why, and how, it all happened. This time her father, Jack, was not just the big bad wolf – his usual role; instead, he made sure she clinched the deal. Unintentionally, Jack Ellis became the matchmaker.

Jack Ellis couldn't believe his good luck when he got a job car cleaning at the Manchester manufacturer of luxury cars, the Imperial Autocar Manufacturing Co. Ltd. based at the Manchester Corporation Company's horse tram depot, close by in Rusholme. Modern day Manchester is not known for making cars but things were different at the turn of the twentieth century. As well as the Imperial Autocar Manufacturing Co. Ltd, Crossleys had also begun to manufacture cars, as had the famous Rolls Royce Engines. In 1904, Ford opened their first factory outside of the USA in Trafford Park, Stretford. By 1938, the car industry in Manchester was in decline, but in the early years Manchester's expertise in engineering, machine-making and innovation made it a flourishing centre of production. At the turn of the century, the automobile was a luxury item *par excellence*; a toy for the rich boy. But the production provided a living for countless workers, not least Jack Ellis. This wasn't car cleaning for a Boy Scout's 'Bob a Job' day. High-quality leather, polished wood, gleaming body work, all demanding exacting standards. Jack lived with his wife Louisa and their two girls, little Louisa and the younger, feistier Mary Ellen. The terraces stretched as far as you could imagine, like a soulless desert of bricks rather than sand, way beyond Rusholme, Moss Side and Ancoats. Back lanes and ginnels separated them with the odd tree or rare green verge. Nothing much had changed in the years since they had been built, apart from the deepening dent in the front steps caused by the fat old woman who knelt worshipping them each day, with a bucket and wire brush. Pride was in short supply and the steps were rare visible evidence of the house-proud wifie. The ironically named Hope Street (probably at best encapsulating a futile aspiration) was no different to the others, save it had Betty's corner shop which was the engine of everyday news and gossip. Betty's was dearer than the Co-op, and you had to forgo the 'divvy', but it was handy and she kept a tab. Most times of the day the same rotund women who had earlier scrubbed their steps and had put their buckets and brushes back in the outhouse, put on their headscarves and waddled along to Betty's to get bread or milk or a bit of sugar, patted butter and some chatter. The latter being worth the hike in price.

Jack Ellis would be the first to admit that he had a temper and occasionally be a bit, shall one say, loose with his fists. He comforted himself by believing he was no worse or better than others on the bloody stupidly named (in this at least Mary Ellen agreed with him) Hope Street or than his pals on the factory floor. Not that loose fists in the home were talked about, far from it, but the men shared a silent understanding; felt, never acknowledged. You can only push a man so far, he would argue. Not much comfort to the bruised Louisa. Mary Ellen had different views, very different views. She determined, with each drunken outburst, that, as soon as she could, she would be off. In the end, it was Jack's bullying that triggered her escape; well, that's how she saw it. *Thank you, Dad, you bastard!*

In truth, the escape had begun some time earlier, well, at least the foundations had been laid. Then the possibilities opened up before her. She had gone with her mother and her sister to Kaye's Fent Warehouse at Brook's Bar. It was on Moss Lane near the Chorlton Road. It was an easy ride on the trolley bus that turned off Moss Lane West. Kaye's was a favourite haunt of her mother's. Old Woolf and Harris and their family had a good eye for material. Thousands of bales or so it seemed, bolts, half rolls and off-cuts stacked on shelves from floor to ceiling. Louisa could turn cheap remnants into clothes. Some she sold, and others were for her and the girls. Mary Ellen had a good eye, too. She picked out more fashionable patterns: tiny flowers in dainty whites and yellows on a pale green background were her favourite at the time. She also had an eye for the lads who worked there. The high stacked warehouse aisles made good hiding places for a side-long glance, a snatched moment to chat. At least it made shopping that bit more interesting, even risqué. Mary Ellen liked that. One of the lads – she never caught his name – caught her eye. Tall and skinny, with a slight possibility of muscly biceps, though well hidden. He was shy and his deep, dark eyes darted down at any sign of contact. But he had seen her, she knew that much. He was a little oriental, a touch mysterious. His untidy beard shaped his long face and proud jaw. He was pale, looked like he needed a bit of feeding up, but dreamy enough. She was not besotted, but she liked the attention and imagined a possibility. It was, in a sense, no more than a shared, fragile meeting of eyes, but enough to promise more. A promise she pondered, a promise that filled her fantasies.

A few weeks later Mary Ellen was walking in Alexandra Park with some friends: Emma Wolstenholme and Sarah Gregson, if her memory was correct. Alexandra Park was a favourite haunt of theirs. It was a favourite haunt of many people, a welcome green space amid the terraces and chimneys, the smog and poverty of Moss Side and Whalley Range. The park was, by any standard, huge, developed by Manchester Corporation when it was bought from William Egerton in 1864. It was designed around two large ovals with wide paths for carriages and swirling extensions excellent for elegant perambulation, but also perfect for girls playing with fancy ideas of courting and romance. There was a bonnie lake at the centre and fields for sport, as well as hedges and small copses of trees with scattered shelters and benches. Above all, there was space, nooks and crannies, with hints of privacy, even intimacy. On any normal day you could find groups of lads and girls playing and teasing each other with their presence. Especially at weekends, though Saturdays less so.

This particular day, a group of lads were kicking a ball around, fooling about. They were laughing and larking in a typical loud laddish way, apparently oblivious to the lasses who watched them. The lads had a foreign look – all were bearded, with longish hair and dark, old-fashioned clothes. They were loud, tumbling and play-fighting over the ball. Mary Ellen asked Emma if she knew them, though she had already clocked who they were. Emma laughed in reply, 'Don't you know? Perhaps you would recognise them at work. They are the Kaye lads from the remnant warehouse in Brook's Bar. The shop is closed on Saturdays. They are Jewish, though people say they are not that religious. They make the most of their day off, away from the stacks of material.'

At that point there was a thud and a bounce as the ball they were kicking hurtled into the group and the girls let out a cry, followed by hysterical giggles. One lad, the lanky one, came over to apologise but perhaps he had another motive; perhaps it was all a set-up? That's what Mary Ellen thought in retrospect. He was shy, averting his deep brown eyes the minute they made a fleeting contact with hers. Then his head lopped to one side, puppy-like, and his long legs became gangly, almost uncoordinated. He wasn't used to girls, that, at least, was obvious. Fortunately, Mary Ellen was not so backward at coming forward.

'Didn't I see you at Kaye's the other day?' she provoked, knowing quite well the answer to her question.

'Probably,' he replied. 'That's where I work.'

That's how it began. Following that supposed accidental meeting, they were often together in the park, walking and talking. She made him laugh. He had never met anyone like her. She was flattered by his attention, loved his eyes, his mysterious quietness, his utter ineptitude in her presence. For both of them it was an escape from their worlds, very different worlds. She couldn't recall how things progressed; the sequence of events was a blur. She forgot the first touch, the first hesitant, lip-brushing kiss, the first attempted fumble. What she remembered was that she had to make all the moves, lead him on, move his hand to gently feel her rounded breast, to touch that nipple which hardened slowly and yearned to be caressed by his damp lips, tickled by his beard. She surprised herself, being so aroused by his naïve fumbling attempts to explore her body. What she liked most, however, was that she was in complete control; she could direct his touch and without much effort she could make him breathless, begging for more. And yet he would never go beyond her leading. So, in any moment she chose, she could stop him, even if he was yearning to find relief. She looked into his puppy dog eyes and laughed to herself. She had this power in her body and at her command. Why, she wondered, had Louisa not wielded it with her father? Why didn't other women on the street look out for themselves when they had an awesome control mechanism in their armour? Probably it was when faced with brute force, she reflected. That is why she liked her gangly Jewish lad from Kaye's.

They lived close to each other but they might have been from different planets, a fact of which they were not ignorant. Perhaps that is what made their growing courtship that bit more exciting. It was secret, a little naughty, it had an edge, was a bit risky, even daring, though in reality it was tame enough. What they had in common was that they were both looking for an escape, some easy transport to somewhere else. They were looking for something different, though it was Mary Ellen who had the determination to take any opportunity by the scruff of the neck. She called him Joe, though she knew it wasn't his real name but then neither was Kaye. He was reinventing himself, and she played along. Changing names was not unusual to him, just as it wasn't unusual to most of his clan. One way of hiding from danger was to become like the rest, so they tweaked a little here and there and came up with something more akin to their neighbours. Of course, it was a guise that failed miserably and Joe soon learnt that escaping your roots needed more than a change in nomenclature. Their worlds were tightly bound cultures, full of signals and rituals, values and habits, that crept upon you, even if you were trying to resist them. Serve him a bacon sandwich and stand back and watch! Suggest she might light the

Sabbath candles and say the table prayers and watch her balk! At least initially these differences were more of interest than concern; besides, they were both looking for a visa to a new world, one they could not explain or even visualise, but one where freedom was more than a weak aspiration.

His family was, in reality, not that committed to their Jewish faith. They connected with the synagogue more because there were others there who spoke the language of their homeland, who cooked the same delicacies, and shared their dreams of settling in a new land. His father explained that life back home was like that too. Their kind of Jewishness was infected with a streak of liberalism, a desire to fit in, rather than, like some of their brethren from other groups, an attempt to turn in on themselves and close the windows (and the doors) to outsiders tight shut. Still, he thought that his courtship with Mary Ellen might cross a line, shock his folks, be just beyond the pale. Yet he remained entranced by her.

She, however, knew exactly the danger she was courting, and that was, if she was honest, part of the attraction. She imagined shocking her father, playing with his simmering anger, showing him he wasn't in control. Her knowledge of Jewishness, or of Judaism, was even less than her knowledge of any religion. She had little interest. Yet you couldn't live in Manchester in the 1920s and not see dark clouds, hear rumours, and try to avoid the violence and the threat. You couldn't live in Manchester and not be aware of the Blackshirts and their violent parades. After all, the family of the founder of the British Union of Fascists, Oswald Mosley, hailed from Manchester. Mosley had taken the title of 6th Baronet Mosley of Ancoats. A major street in the town centre bore the Mosley family name. Joe and Mary Ellen's blossoming courtship was before the terrible riots at the Free Trade Hall, and the later infamous Battle of Cable Street, but it was in Broughton that the burgeoning BUF had its Northern headquarters. Much of this detail would be lost on Mary Ellen, but she knew of the marches and the threats. She knew that a favourite café of the Blackshirts was near Victoria Station and the Blackshirts would gather there and parade through Strangeways, along Bury

New Road, just to provoke the local Jewish communities. She knew enough to recognise that her relationship with Joe was playing with fire. She found that she liked it hot.

It would be hard to trace when the next phase of the plan became openly spoken about, or by whom. In one sense, it was a young couple naively dreaming of a love-filled utopia. Yet this was not a soapy version of a contemporary Romeo and Juliet. Rather, in a real sense it was two young people searching for an exit plan from their trapped lives. They would run away, they would get a flat, they would get married. It was as easy as that, or so they thought. However, dreams can sometimes burst into reality, even if they would turn out to be less enticing or sustaining as they had seemed at the time. She bided her time, for sure, but she worked on Joe. She built up his dreams.

'Why not finish the new name business?'

'We could choose a new surname as well.'

'Look for a furnished flat or some rooms.'

Joe was excited but wary.

'What about our parents? They'll go ballistic!'

'Then we shouldn't ask, just get on with it,' she replied.

Now she had planted the idea and so she watched it grow and grow.

*

The end of any week was always a dangerous time in the Ellis house in 'Despair Street' (that's what she had decided to call it). Jack rolled through the door full of expletives. Red-faced and blue-nosed. He needed food – *now!*

'Now!' he repeated as he banged his fists on the table. The three women watched those fists; they looked for where they may fly next. Louisa served him food and tried to calm him but he had drunk too much. In a single swipe, he cleared the table; food, crockery and cutlery flew in every direction. The sound was worse than the broken shards that somehow they had managed to avoid.

'I said *food*, woman! Not that shit! Can't you cook, or is it just that you won't? You ungrateful witch!'

Louisa by this time was cowering in a corner.

'Get out, you two, go now!' she cried.

'But, but what about you …?' they screamed.

'Just get the hell out!' she shouted, allowing them no time to finish their sentence. By this time, Jack was lurching heavily towards Lou. She could, at least for a moment, duck and dive but soon his fist landed on her head and she fell. Then, as she curled in a ball on the floor, he kicked out.

'Let it finish!' she prayed as the pain spread through her body. 'He can't help it, it's the drink working its wicked way, he will be all sorry in the morning.'

A stream of thoughts went through her mind as she tried to breathe through the pain. It was as if she was in labour again, each hit a new contraction. Except the tears did not come from a new life; they were just part of an old life repeating its terrors. The end came when he vomited over her. Vile, beer-smelling, green vomit. With a last wretch, he slumped, drained and exhausted, onto the settee. Now she looked at him sleeping like a baby, mouth wide open, snoring, vomit dripping around his nose and lips. She struggled to get up. Staggering, she found an old tea towel, wet it, and began to wipe herself down. The girls came in with her sister and looked at the mess. The disaster on the floor – crockery shards, food and cutlery everywhere. More importantly the disaster that was Lou, bloodstained and bent double.

'I'll be alright,' she declared. Then she recounted those thoughts she had used to distract herself from each blow until she buckled. 'He'll be all apologies tomorrow, to be sure,' she whispered through wet eyes and a blood-smeared face.

'You always say that, Lou. But one day he'll go too far,' her sister replied. 'It's too much, too much, you don't deserve it.'

This was the trigger, the starting pistol sounding in Mary Ellen's ear, pushing her to make the next move in the exit plan; this was the snowflake that broke the branch, if you like, though a grubby snowflake on pee-stained snow. Now things with Joe moved at a pace; she pushed and nudged just that bit more. They found a furnished flat in Poynton Street, in Chorlton on Medlock. They went to the Registrar's and booked a date for four weeks' time. They chose a new name for Joe. From now on he would be Joe Daniels. That was to be her husband's name: lanky, floppy, dreamy Joe Daniels. They copied the surname from that of some friends, in fact, the only ones they let in on their secret wedding and who would become their witnesses at the Registry. They said nothing to anyone else for the four weeks leading up to the day. Mary Ellen couldn't wait to wave that marriage certificate in her father's sweaty, bulbous face and watch the balloon go up.

*

The wedding was not much of an affair, not an 'affair' at all. It was clinical, almost business-like, and afterwards they rushed to sign the lease for Poynton Street. The happily married couple! All they had to do now was tell Harris and Rose, Jack and Lou. As easy as that. In fact, she was looking forward to telling her parents but she was unsure how to approach the Kayes. She was worried how they might react to the deception, the name changes. Too late now, too late, she told herself. She put on her best dress and shoes, some lipstick and rouge, and brushed her hair. Then the feisty Mary Ellen stepped forward, ready to face the world.

9

Simon Israel: a lap dog with no tail to wag

Simon: from the Hebrew meaning 'listen' or 'hearing'

He wasn't the simmering silent type,
He would just rather wait and let others talk.
Simon knew why he had two ears and only one mouth.
He had learnt the difference between
hearing and listening.

I so wanted to be Joe Daniels, honestly, believe me, but who *was* Joe Daniels? A mere fiction of my introverted, warped imagination, that's who. I had no real idea of how he looked, how he should dress, even less how he thought. In some ways, he was everything Simon wasn't. I had got that far, then I got stuck. It was more difficult than just shaving off my beard, yet the beard was the only bit that Mary Ellen liked. And I forgot, of course, my eyes, my dark eyes. Perhaps the hair and the eyes were the only good things I passed on to Maurice. She would agree with that, I don't doubt. Though she allowed me very little opportunity intentionally pass on much else. I guess there would be stuff in the genes that he got, whether or not she or him liked it.

It wasn't that I hated my family. How could you hate them? Besides, the more you hated *Abba* and *Mame*, the more they loved you, or the more they showed you love. *Mame* drowned you in kindness, that was her way. They had taken many risks to get this far, more than we ever understood. *Abba* worked hard, and he was a good tailor with an eye for material. He was a respected businessman, and the shop was doing well. He made sure of that. In fact, it was doing well enough to support us all. My problem, if that's what you would call it, was that I didn't know how to rebel. I didn't know how to mess about, have fun, *be* fun. Of course, I was one of the lads. I could kick a ball, defend myself, laugh at a joke. But it was hard work for me. Simon would have preferred to curl up in a ball, to hide his face. Simon preferred to listen than to make the joke, wait until he was asked, or chosen, before he joined in the game. Some people thought that made me surly, others said I was fine, simmering or too self-sufficient. None of that was true or right. I think I was frightened, tongue-tied, always ready to run. Mary Ellen talked about my eyes all the time, but what she failed to notice was that they were always on the move because they didn't know where to look. That the pupils were wide because most of the time I was scared of what might happen next. It wasn't that I was expecting anything bad, I just somehow failed to read the runes, so I stayed on high alert. Except in those first few weeks after we met. They were different, I was different, if just fleetingly. As usual, I am getting ahead of myself.

You will guess that she had already caught my eye in the shop. She came in with her mother and her sister. They spent ages wandering up and down the aisles, feeling the cloth, rolling out bail upon bail of material. I think it was a day out for them, an Aladdin's cave of cloth treasure. They did usually buy some pieces, but they looked at far more than they could ever have bought. Mary Ellen had a very definite eye for colours and patterns. She was constantly advising her mother which material would make the best blouses or dresses and what style she imagined them cut into. I watched from behind the stacks of material, staying in the shadow, mesmerised by her confidence, I suppose her brazen manner, her red lips and legs adorned with shiny silken stockings with a tantalising hint of a garter at the. I had never seen anyone like her, and I couldn't stop looking. Just occasionally, very occasionally, she glanced my way, and our eyes met, and I thought (or was it fantasised?) that she smiled. I guess I was smitten, like a lap dog with no tail to wag.

The other lads liked her too but they had spotted my special interest and used it to taunt me. It became a joke in the warehouse, an easy way to watch me redden, to make me wish for a proverbial hole to swallow me up. And the more I blushed, the more they ribbed, the more the game became an obsession. I was trapped, a prisoner of my adolescent hormones and Mary Ellen's flirting.

I remember the day we saw her with the other girls in the park. The others lads knew that I was looking, and the girls were giggling coyly in a huddle. Jacob kicked the ball so that it landed in the middle of them. Without thinking, I rushed over to apologise; it was an instinct, though I should have realised that Jacob was a good shot and I was being set up. That was the first time we – Mary Ellen and I – ever spoke. I was hooked.

After that, I would find any excuse to go the park and see if she was around, and often she was, sometimes on her own too. We walked around the lake, sat in the shelter and talking became something more. I was clumsy, inexperienced, but eager. She led the way, all the way. Looking back, she knew just how to nudge, tease and even direct. My inexperience, my coyness made me easy prey, too easy. Putty in her hands, material waiting to be cut and stitched up.

There was a huge risk in what was happening; perhaps I liked that – she certainly did. The shy, immature lanky Jew boy and the brazen Gentile girl walking out together. The lads back at the warehouse wouldn't believe me if I told them what was happening. For once I would be the centre of attention; they would want me to regale every sordid detail. They would listen, like dogs around a bitch on heat. I would not give them that pleasure. Never. This was *my* adventure, *my* vortex in which to slip. Deeper and deeper, darker and darker.

10

Mother Love

Rose, Rosa, Roisa, Rhoda: Rosa is a Hebrew name that means 'rose', a flower that is known for its beauty and fragility. In Jewish culture, the rose is also associated with love and passion, making Rosa a romantic and poetic name. Over time, the name Rosa has become popular in Jewish communities around the world.

She is the Rose of Sharon, the fairest of the fair.
She bears an aroma of hope,
A balm that comforts
A beauty that inspires
A love that blossoms
A quiet, determined dust of peace.

Mary Ellen shook Joe by the shoulders.

'Breathe deep. Be a real man,' she said. 'We'll start at mine and I will show you how it's done. Smile! It will be fine!'

She marched, war-like, to the front door of the house in 'Despair Street', with Joe clinging to her for dear life. Her sister answered and recoiled, a bit shaken. Mary Ellen was taking no prisoners and continued her progression through into the back kitchen. An almost familiar scene met her and Joe. Her father sat in his chair in the corner near the fire, her mother banging plates in the scullery. She came almost immediately through to the room, wiping her hands nervously on her dark, crinkled pinny. Jack didn't give her eye contact.

'Where have you been, Mary Ellen? We have been worried to death. Haven't we, Jack?' said Lou.

'Couldn't give a pig's trotter, meself. How about you, Jew boy? Would you give a pig's trotter?' a gruff Jack spoke into the air before fixing his menacing eyes on the lad before him.

There was a silence. A disturbing silence, but Mary Ellen was not one for backing off. It was time to get the job done, done and dusted.

'Well, you might as well get the whole story. This is Joe Daniels, my husband,' she brazenly declared. At which point she waved her left hand so they could glimpse the slim band of gold on her fourth finger.

Her mother let out a loud haunting shriek which seemed to continue for ever. Now Jack stood up, slowly but firmly, on to two feet. He turned towards them his full reddened face.

'Shut up, woman! I've had enough of your melodramatics!' he grunted to Lou. 'Go upstairs get her stuff and throw it out of the window. Louise, help your ma.'

Then he turned to Mary Ellen and Jo.

'You two get out of my house, you are not welcome here! Get out, girl, get out and take that dirty fucking Jew with you. Don't come back, do you hear me? Don't ever come back, you bitch!'

Mary Ellen had made her point, she had nothing to add. She grabbed Joe and headed to the door; she knew what happened next. She had seen it all before. Now he would explode. Hopefully, he would hit the wall, not Louisa, but that was not her problem now. On the street, her clothes and shoes flapped down in the wind from the open window, landing strewn on the pavement and the kerbs. Curtains twitched and doors slowly opened.

'Come out and see, you nosy buggers! Don't miss the bloody spectacle! A free show!' she screamed.

Joe looked frightened to death. He bent to pick up a discarded blouse.

'Leave them, Joe, leave them for the bloody scavengers. Here you are, Ma Arkright, see if this fits your fat arse! How about you, Fanny, this might help you with your fancy man, and the milkman on his usual rounds. Emma, you always wanted my stuff and now you can have it, gratis. It won't improve your chances, you need to get rid of the scabs first. Oh, we all know the secrets, the secrets of bloody Hope Street. I'm out of here for good. Thank God!'

They left the street, hand in hand. Mary Ellen turned just once to see her mother and her sister staring out of the window. They looked like they might have been waving. The look in their eyes haunted her. Pathetic.

Mary Ellen was fired up now. She could take on the world. Joe quaked as they made their way to Moss Lane to the home of Harris and Rose Karavitch. Entering their house was like entering an alternative world. It was dark, with drapes on the chairs and the table, in the middle of which stood a large candlestick. Rose was dressed in grey, long clothing, her head and hair covered in a scarf that was tied at the back. She moved peacefully, quietly to welcome them in.

'Simon, we have been worried about you. Where have you been? Introduce me to your friend.'

'I am so sorry, *Mame*, this is Mary Ellen. Is *Abba* home? Would he… he speak with me?'

'Of course, Simon. I will call him from his study. He is, as always, doing his accounts, always his accounts.'

The door to the room opened and a slim, wiry man quietly entered. He had a long, tidy, wiry beard, a small cap on his head and a long coat around him tied in the middle.

'Blessed be G-d! It is you, dear Simon! Your mother and I have been beside ourselves. Come, my boy, sit down and bring this young lady with you. We should talk. Your mother will make us some coffee I am sure, won't you, *Mame*?'

He pulled out some chairs and beckoned them to sit around the table. Mary Ellen sat, feeling her heart continue to beat fast, rhythmic, but her fire, the fire in her belly, drained away from her. She felt faint. It was too peaceful, too calm, she was unnerved, at a loss how to behave. Suddenly she felt overdressed, brassy, immodest, loud. She wanted to wipe away the lipstick and the rouge, cover her hair. Instead, she lowered her head. It was Joe who had to handle this. She hated to admit it but she was out of her depth. She was almost begging this elderly man to get angry, to shout, to follow her father's example and throw them out. But she knew that wasn't going to happen. He lit the candles.

'It's not sabbath but candlelight might help,' he said. 'Don't shake, Simon, this is your *abba*, talk to me. We can work this out, whatever you bring to us. Now introduce me to this beautiful young lady.'

Rose brought in the coffee, strong smelling and black. Mary Ellen had never tasted anything like it; she had only ever seen bottles of Camp coffee, a syrupy concoction that she rarely drank. Joe now developed a stutter, but with some encouragement, he got through. He explained all that had happened.

'Oh, my dear Simon, what a pickle you have got yourselves into! Is this marriage what you want? Is this what you want too, Mary Ellen?'

Sheepishly, they both nodded.

'Then you must do your best to make it good. It will not be easy for you both. Marriage is never easy, but one built on strange names and which joins two cultures will have its own peculiar difficulties. Mary Ellen will not be used to our ways, not used to the way people treat us. You will have to learn hers, too. But you will have my blessing, always. Now you must take responsibility for your new wife. *Mame*, I think you should call our family to join us and we will have a glass of vodka together. We must help turn this time from sadness to celebration. Our son is married to the beautiful Miriam.'

Joe's mother gathered her brood and they found chairs in the room. There was a blazing fire and the candles flickered, making a warm, moving glow. It was an alien country to Mary Ellen; she was quiet, disarmed, almost reserved. A first for her. Joe's father had found a way to pour calm on her burning anger; there was nothing to fight for and she was at a loss of what to do.

She accepted the small glass of vodka as Harris raised a toast to the newly-wed Karavitches, or the Daniels – Harris wasn't sure which was best, but he seemed happy with either. Immediately, he started to sing. It was an old folk song from back home but the whole family knew it, and one by one they joined in the chorus. Joe smiled, that shy grin that made his eyes sparkle.

'Miriam – may I call you that? It is Mary in our language, and Simon Israel – or should I say Joe now? Today we call upon the Almighty to bless you both. *Bah-rookh ah-tah ah-doh-noi eh-loh-hay-noo meh-lekh hah-oh-lahm boh-ray peh-ree hah-gah-fehn.* (Blessed are You, L-rd our G-d, King of the universe, who creates the fruit of the vine.)

And so, he continued with all seven blessings of the *Sheva Brachot*. The whole family listened in silence and cheered as he raised his second glass.

'I remember the day we got married. It was a village affair, we had little money but much merriment. Your Baboo Schimanski made the most delicious chicken soup – not as good as *Mame's*, of course,' he quickly added. 'That day I think she fed the whole of Suwałki. *Mame*, do you remember the *flodni* [layered pastry with apples, walnuts, currants and poppy seeds]? It was to die for! My mouth waters at the thought of it. You must make some for us Rose, when you have time, my dear. They were difficult times but we had happy moments too, none more so than on the day we stood under the *Chuppah* together.'

The evening moved steadily on with much laughter and many stories of Rudamina and Suwałki. For Mary Ellen, it was pleasure mixed with sheer torture. She couldn't bear to see them so happy together. She was crying inside, begging for Harris to shout and be angry. What had she done? She wanted freedom, not cosy family; risk, not kindness and compassion; to escape *from*, not *into* a new world she didn't understand or even begin to know how to navigate. A world where her feistiness seemed to carry no truck. She knew she had lost, but it was a battle for which she was ill-prepared. She had no weapons in her arsenal to bring to bear. How could she stand up and growl at the kindly Harris? How could she upset the sweet and gentle Rose? How could she destroy her shy Joe and drag him from his place, his home, his people? At least by now the vodka was having an effect. She could smile and laugh at their memories, their collective nostalgia, as if she understood the meaning. She could flirt just a little with Nathan; he was more chirpy, cheeky and alive than his older brother, Jacob. The girls (Fanny, Yetta, Sybil, Annie, Dora, Golda), too many to remember all their names, giggled and smiled and cooed over her dress and make-up. It was as if they were dragging her in, strange as she was to them. For Mary Ellen, it was as if they were sucking the life out of her and spewing it up in their candle-lit parlour.

'I am so happy, so blessed,' sang Harris. 'I thought I had lost my precious son but now I have gained a beautiful daughter. Praise be.' He paused for a moment. 'You will come on Friday, you will welcome the sweet Sabbath with us. Please. We promise chicken soup and *flodni*, don't we, *Mame*?'

So, they went out into the black, dank night to catch the trolley bus back to Chorlton. To their rooms without a fire, or flickering candles, or grinning teeth. Joe was euphoric and she tried to be, though in truth her heart was not in it. She had begun an adventure for which she was ill-prepared and had little enthusiasm.

Over the next few weeks and months, Mary Ellen tried, she really tried, to find a place with them, a place she could accept. She couldn't find fault. The welcome among the family continued ad nauseum. Joe kept his new name and his job at the shop. She endured Sabbath evenings which were way beyond her understanding and interest but she feigned enthusiasm. Kosher food was a mystery she couldn't be bothered with – no milk or dairy with meat, specially killed animals for meat. She had never eaten shellfish so she didn't miss much. However, she drew a line at not having bacon butties, much to Joe's quiet disgust. All in all, she felt cramped by kindness. She was in a prison of cosiness which she hated as much as the violence of her own family from which she had escaped. Most of all, Joe's father had skilfully, disarmed and domesticated her feistiness. With one foul stroke, he had made her rebellious spirit pointless, meaningless, an utter waste of energy. Slowly it strangled her relationship with Joe. They were no longer naughty, they were no longer taking risks, their togetherness had no edge. The lioness was caged if not yet quite domesticated.

Fortunately, at least for a while, there was one silver lining to the ominous cloud of normality. Harris suggested she might join them working in the shop. He noticed her eye for pretty material, her understanding of dressmaking thanks to her mother's tuition. She loved it. Handling the cotton prints, helping to choose the latest bails, guessing what might trend. She liked, most of all, estimating the profit margins. There was a business woman lurking there somewhere.

The inevitable happened. Mary Ellen knew that she was pregnant. If she was honest, it wasn't the first time but she didn't tell Joe. Her determination to marry him was partly driven by an earlier pregnancy but she had miscarried. Maybe that would happen this time. She was not too bothered either way. She was learning to use whatever happened to some kind of advantage. Though she was also learning that to do that, you had to be malleable, adaptive in your goals. She would keep her options open.

Joe on the other hand seemed to be enjoying domesticity. He had what he wanted: a wife who was that little bit different, and brash enough to push him out of his comfort zone. A trophy among his Jewish peers. Also, he had managed to have got all this without losing his family connections or support. As a prospective dad, he was over the moon, deliriously, pathetically so. Mary Ellen was tempted to say that all his Christmases had come at once but she had learnt that wouldn't work for Joe. Would 'all his Chanukahs' have the same effect? Who knew? Who cared? She was finding this religious stuff tedious. What surprised her most was that they weren't really a religious family, they just did all this 'weird stuff'. But she reflected that was true of the Ellis family, who every year decorated a tree and tucked into turkey – if they could afford it. Well, even if they couldn't afford it, Jack still made it a good excuse to get drunk and throw a fist or two. Usually in her mum's direction. At least Chanukah spared her that.

Harris and Rose shared in Joe's joy. It would be their first grandchild, an honour, though they knew the child would not be a thoroughbred Jew. But they did not falter in their joy or pride. Mary Ellen accepted that they knew exactly how to reign her in: smother her with kindness. It was boringly, annoyingly claustrophobic, but for now she had no alternative. She would smile through gritted teeth and pay the dutiful *takhter* (daughter-in-law), though remain stubbornly *goy*.

This time the pregnancy progressed without difficulty. She couldn't say she enjoyed it but she enjoyed the fuss from those all around, not least her Yiddish family. No doubt there would be traditions to follow, bizarre customs to endure but she was getting used to that. Her strategy was to go along with things and, at some point, put a marker down. She would carefully draw a line, and test again that sickening kindness with which they were slowly draining the life from her.

In the meantime, as she grew rounder, she relished working in the warehouse. There was one memorable day when she saw her mother and Louisa come to buy some material. Louisa was obviously on a sewing spree. She saw them way before they saw her and she managed to dodge front-of-house and avoid them. She was never sure whether they had made the connection with Kaye's Fents Warehouse and Joe. They had, after all, only seen him with her that one memorable night. Her last memory was the two of them staring at her from the bedroom window, her clothes strewn all over the street as she left. She wondered if their pitiful looks were of sadness or envy. She had escaped. Now she realised prisons came in different forms and even kindly ones could be claustrophobic.

When her time came, Rose and the sisters rallied round. More chicken soup was made, though Mary didn't have any. Joe probably needed it more than her. He waited nervously, agitated, unable to stay still. Thank God he was eventually shooed away. Rose was a skilled 'shooer' of men, and just the women were left to oversee the business. She remembered little except the pain and the first cry. Perhaps that was enough. The baby was like a battered purple prune except for a mop of dark hair and a loud pair of lungs. She held him, somewhat mesmerised. She would never have called herself the maternal type. Now she looked at this scraggy thing and wondered if maternal feelings would somehow just happen, appear from nowhere. If those feelings would fill up the space left by the baby, and the afterbirth that had grown inside her and had now escaped her still-bloated belly. For now, she was too tired to care. In a dreamlike sequence, she fed the boy and handed him to Joe. He cried, as did Joe's mother and old Harris. They mumbled something in Hebrew or Yiddish in each of the boy's ears; she could never get the hang of this mumbo jumbo. It would be some superstition or prayer. She had grown to care little and to let them get on with it. For a moment, a fleeting moment, she missed her own mother. But she pushed that thought, that feeling, as far down as she could. She breathed deeply. Hormones aside, she refused to get soppy and sentimental. Now with the baby she was trapped even more than before. Not only the Karavitches but this little mite would suck her life away.

The next few days were a blur but she knew that things would be happening behind the scenes. She forced herself to not only take an interest, but to keep some control. A name? What would they call him? She put her foot down, demanding that he must be registered as a Daniels and his father as Joe. Her boy would not have to search for an anglicised name. She agreed to the name Maurice; she thought it had a certain air to it – she didn't know it was of French origin. For Joe, Rose and Harris it was Moses or Moshe with an English twist. Just like Harris was a variant of Hirsch. For them, names mattered, though they were always ready to change them or add others. His Hebrew name would be Moshe ben Simon and they would use that at the *B'rt Milah*, whatever that was. All she knew was that it was circumcision, and she had reluctantly agreed to it, though she warned Joe there would be no other Jewish mumbo jumbo – or any other religious stuff. That would be it. With a full stop. Joe smiled, anything to please her, and Harris and Rose were glad that they had got this far without trouble.

The rest happened quickly, so quickly she could hardly get her head around it. Eight days later, they gathered in the Karavitch home in Moss Lane. Rose and the girls had cooked a feast, a Jewish one. They paid for a man (a *mohel*) to do the business. It seemed pretty gruesome to Mary Ellen but she was assured it would not hurt the little scrag that she held in her arms. Joe got one of his friends, one of the *real* Daniels, who had witnessed their marriage, to be the official *sandek*, kind of like a godfather at a baptism but with more blood! Maurice cried but soon settled. The rest was lost in a vodka blur. At least she had got a taste for the vodka. Meanwhile, Joe was walking on air. Soon they were singing again and soon she escaped to feed the baby and leave them to their mysterious, tedious, boring celebrations. She was glad to get back to Chorlton and their spartan flat.

She didn't get into work for a while, but no one bothered. She was the queen of the home now and she intended to make the most of it. She all too easily became bored, but she found a new routine. She began to take up with some old school friends; they were curious and jealous. She liked that mix. Of course, they didn't know the truth: the truth about what she felt about Joe now that he had lost any mystery. They didn't know what it was like to be an appendage, a trophy if you will, to a Jewish family, even if they weren't a religious one. A family that couldn't separate their old country practices from the demands of Judaism, and she couldn't help them. Sometimes she thought that they saw her as proof that they had finally become British. She knew that this Jewishness wasn't her scene; if truth be told, it bored her to death. She wondered how long she could hide her ennui without it turning in to hate, and bursting like a popped boil.

Maurice grew, fat at first, but when he started crawling he lost a bit of that childlike chubbiness. He was dark, scrawny now, and fast. His skin not quite olive but almost, and his hair a real mop of jet black. Most of all you could see the Karavitch in him, in his deep, dark brown eyes. They shone sometimes like alien stars and other times they pierced whoever he looked at. Joe was transfixed. Mary Ellen was as yet unsure whether to follow the pull of the maternal strings or see them as chains, an inescapable link to a future she was fast wishing wasn't hers.

She met Walter Miller through an old school friend. It was her first foray into the world outside the Karavitch family bubble. She wasn't sure what to make of Walter at first. He was one of a crowd but the two of them connected at some deeper level. Joe met the crowd once or twice. At the time, Walter was courting Teresa Green, a friend of Mary Ellen's best school pal, Ethel. They all hung about together like school kids at break. On a few nights, Harris and Rose would take Maurice, and she and Joe joined the crowd at the pictures and once at the George & Dragon on Ardwick Green. Joe had never been in a pub before and was all at sea, but he went along with it. He even tried a pint of mild, though he said he preferred neat vodka. He was less keen on trying cigarettes but Mary Ellen enjoyed them from the very first drag. It had been a long time since she had been so carefree and almost wanton. It was addictive and she found the floundering Joe amusing, like a plaything. It softened, for a dull moment, her growing despising of this lanky, awkward, pitiful lad she had married to escape a boring life – only to find she was caught in an alternative one. More benign, of course, but equally trapping. She had been imprisoned by a Jewish homeliness and a dollop of kindliness that was slowly smothering her.

She would go back to the George & Dragon on a few occasions, sometimes now without Joe. The crowd were regulars, and for her it was an escape to her kind of normality. Joe accepted she needed space away from the all-consuming Karavitch culture. He knew that feeling only too well, though since he had Mary Ellen, and then the arrival of Maurice, it had dissipated, just plain gone. He might feel awkward in the George & Dragon but at home he felt somehow alright, settled, content. Had he found his place, or was it just the settling of a young man's hormones? Who knows. He hoped that it would one day be the same for Mary Ellen, but he knew that wasn't the case at the moment. She seemed fine for a while and then something almost reckless burst out, and she craved her *goy* life. She rebelled against anything alien, anything Jewish, that demanded her attention. He recognised that not even with Maurice was she going to simply settle. It was a constant nagging, a worry, but there was little he could do. So, he let her go to meet her friends; perhaps it would work its way out of her system. A risk he had no option but to quietly embrace.

Sometimes Joe would continue to join them but Mary Ellen knew he hated it, and so did everyone else. It was painful, and usually spoilt the night, or made her more outrageous, more defiant. It would end with the nearest Joe could get to an argument. Sulking silence! Like her dad used to say, 'He has th'monk on!' and it could last for a while. She couldn't really remember why it happened or what she had said or done; probably she was either a little drunk or angry. Perhaps she had done something to shock herself, to rediscover the old feisty, feral Mary Ellen. Whatever, it started to happen more and more frequently.

She had noticed Walter's glances, his hanging around. Teresa Green had disappeared with the summer; Mary Ellen saw it as pun on her name. It was autumn at least, but for Teresa more like winter! 'No more 'trees are green,' she smirked to herself. One evening, Walter sat next to her and they chatted for most of the night. She couldn't tell you what they chatted about but it made her laugh. An old feeling crept up on her unawares. A slight adrenalin rush at first but the juices that trickled then began to flow, and she started not to care, not even to think about it, to just be in the moment. Joe became a faint, distant voice in the back of her head, a pathetic attempt to prick her conscience. Walter kept talking, talking louder. She laughed. The rest just happened. Looking back, it was as cheap and seedy as it was deceitful. She abandoned herself and refused to accept any shame. That was her style after all; she would make no excuses; she was free, or she thought she was at that moment, at least.

Soon, she was meeting Walter regularly, whenever she could get a way. Harris and Rose were always ready to babysit. Doting Yiddish grandparents had their uses. She just had to keep finding excuses to be out. She knew it couldn't go on for ever. Sooner or later, something would break, usually her. But until it did, she enjoyed her free thinking, her free-wheeling, without much thought or an ounce of regret.

In the end, she took a coward's way out. Some would say it was cold, callous. 'They can say what the hell they like,' she thought to herself. She had begun to despise Joe Daniels. His dark twinkling eyes had become black dots of fear, his beard was now straggly and unkempt, his legs gangly and uncoordinated, his pallor as grey and weak as his spine. What had she seen in him? God only knew. He wasn't worth the fight, he would simply scrunch up in a frightened ball, pleading to be played with, taunted, and she didn't have the energy, it wasn't fun anymore. This cat had lost interest in the ball of yarn, she had scratched it too much and now she had found a new scraping post. The Karavitches didn't fare much better in her mind's eye. She'd had enough of their piety, their simple ways, the killing her with kindness. She needed some passion, not prayers with candles, some life, not mumbo jumbo with Yiddish ditties. She preferred being back with her own sort. Then, and only then, could she become queen of her castle, mistress of all that surrounded her plump frame. She had escaped once, and she would do it again. Besides, she knew that sooner or later she would be caught. Intimacy with Joe had long since gone and if she fell pregnant, it would be all too clear that it wasn't Joe who'd managed to issue another child. She somehow even enjoyed the risk of waiting each month for the sickness and the lateness. The one, perhaps only one, thing that got in the way was Maurice. Where did he fit in to the equation, other than the fact he caused a stumbling block? The only pawn in the game that checked her moves.

At one point she considered just leaving him with them. It would be the easiest decision or the one that would cause least hassle. Harris and Rose were besotted with him, he would be safe in their care. On the other hand, other grandchildren were on the way. No doubt many more would follow. They bred well, the Karavitchs. Maurice would always only be a half breed, never a true member of the clan. Joe loved him, of that she was sure, but he loved her too and look how boring that was. Could she leave this little mite to a life of 'scissors and ironing boards'? Not a chance in hell. It was a nuisance but he would have to come with her, the only responsibility she would take, no matter how much it irked her. It was worrying; she was getting soft and maternal. She would have to reign that in.

She decided to push Walter, nudge him with a little Mary Ellen panache. It was time to make a move and he was integral to the plan. Walter was putty in her hands, she could wrap him round her little finger without even mentioning any possibilities of a pregnancy. A hint was enough and she could keep the real thing as a back-up plan, keep possible pregnancy as a get out of jail card. She soon had Walter scurrying around for a flat, or some rooms, that they could move into. They (or it) had to be not too far away but far enough to give her some safe distance from the Karavitches and Joe. She would refuse to go into hiding but she needed enough space to think and not be under constant surveillance.

Walter moved quicker than she thought possible. The rooms in Gorton near Belle Vue were not great but they would do. Walter worked for the Council, his pay wasn't large but they would manage for now. She would think of something to enhance their income; a bit of creativity would work. She wanted everything in place for when she told Joe. She would have to leave the minute Joe knew what had been happening and she had to take Maurice. No hesitation or prevarication – that just made for complications or prolonged any agony. It had to be quick and clean like the scissor cut of a master tailor or, in this case, a mistress tailor!

Once she had seen the rooms and approved them, she packed her cases, well bags really, but she made do. This time she was taking her stuff with her. That evening she waited, ready. She heard the key in the lock. Joe had finished his shift at the warehouse; it would be him. She picked up Maurice. By now, Joe would have seen the bags at the door. He came into the room.

'Is something wrong, Mary?' His eyes would not meet hers, his head lolloped to one side.

'It's time Joe. You have been expecting this, I know. It just isn't working for me or you. Time, I moved on.'

'Just like that? Just like that! My God, how can you? Stop! Just like that? What about the lad? What about us?'

'Joe, we have had our time, but it's best to cut clean. You'll be better off, I promise.'

She reached up and pecked him on the cheek and left. She didn't look back; she couldn't this time. But the child did. She carried him on her shoulder; she couldn't see his tears; she didn't look at his tiny hand waving at his father in that closed-fisted baby way. She shut her ears to his whisper, '*Abba*,' but Joe saw and heard, and wept, deep in his heart.

*

The rooms that Walter had secured were not up to much but there were no tawdry drapes or religious babble for once, no flickering candles or smarmy, peaceful kindness filling the air, causing her to struggle for breath. Just Walter, her and the kid. Maurice was more of a trouble than she'd thought, now she was trapped in Gorton of all places. Here, there were no easy babysitters on hand. Now she had the little one all the time, no relief. But pride made sure that she didn't ask the Karavitches for any help. She never saw them again, she never even tried to, she had moved on. Snip, cut and leave someone else to sew up the weeping wounds. They were the tailors, after all.

Joe was beaten, humiliated, destroyed. Joe Daniels died that day; it was Simon who returned to the family home; it was Simon who cancelled the lease; Simon who carried their few remaining possessions out of the damp dreary rooms; Simon, a crumpled, pathetic figure, who knocked on the door at Moss Lane and fell weeping into his mother's waiting arms.

The family pulled around him in a comforting huddle. No one thought to say, 'We told you so,' or if they did, they remained silent. The whole family wept for him, wept for themselves. They had tried to welcome 'Miriam' into their fold. Above all, they mourned the loss of Maurice. Rose and the girls had doted on him, cooed over his antics and babbling. They had changed his nappies, bathed and fed him. Mary Ellen had mesmerised them, it was like she was from a different planet. Her clothes, her make-up, the way she talked and even her posture were at the same time shocking and alluring. Now, perhaps inevitably, she had dropped them like a brick. Simon had been captured by her, hook, line and sinker, absolutely completely, and the rest of them hadn't been far behind. His fall would be hard. She had left the shy, lanky, gentle, mesmerised Joe Daniels broken, bereft.

He moved back to Moss Lane where Rose fed him chicken soup and love. His sisters dallied around him and his brothers rallied, especially Nathan. *Abba* was, as always, gentle, but also firm. His wisdom would prevail. *It's time to let go, Simon. We will be with you, come back home, where you belong.*

Simon struggled, his eyes downcast, his walk sad and slumped. He tried to see the boy once, walked off with the pram, but Rose saw him and made sure Maurice was returned. Mary Ellen made it clear he was to have no contact whatsoever. Rose and Harris convinced him it was in the end for the best, for him and more importantly for Maurice.

'You must not play games with a child's life. Let his mother do what she thinks is best.'

So, when Mary Ellen changed the boy's name, Joe and Maurice were both erased completely. Just as if they had never happened. But Simon knew that was not the real case. He never gave up hoping; he remembered the little hand waving goodbye. Slowly, Simon grew that bit stronger but he would always be hurt, scarred inside. Never again could he give himself to anyone. He would tramp through life, unable to lift his head or look another in the eye. If he ached for anything, it was for his son. He would have given the world to hear him say *Abba* again, just once would have been enough. But he never did.

1931 was a strange year for Simon Karavitch, for all the Karavitches. In one sense, it was terrible and tragic. It was the year that Harris died. It was more than a shock. The family were bereft. It took Rose to hold them all together, to hold herself together. Fortunately, *Abba's* presence lingered. Uncle Woolf met with them and they decided that they would carry on together with the Fent Warehouse, which Harris and Woolf had built up together. It would provide an income for Rose and jobs for the family. It was also a year of new beginnings, when Nathan decided that it was time to stand on his own. He was blessed with the Karavitch spirit of entrepreneurism. He opened a small fresh fruit and fish shop. Later, Simon would join him, but Jacob, the eldest brother, and the girls stayed working at the warehouse.

It was in the late autumn that Mary Ellen played a new card. She wrote to Simon, well, she didn't but her solicitor did, to say she wanted to get married to Walter Miller. She was now pregnant with his child. Simon was unable to cope with this. It felt like a final bond with Maurice was being cut. He couldn't bear it. He wouldn't speak, just curled into himself. He became silent and tortured. He would not forgive himself and remained a prisoner of his sadness. Nathan, supported by Uncle Woolf, took matters into their hands. They arranged for Simon to file for divorce and name Walter as corespondent. They persuaded Simon to put the whole episode behind him once and for all. He needed to cut loose from the hold it had on him. He understood, he had no option, but it had destroyed him in ways he would never recover from. Rose's heart wept for him as much as it did for her beloved Harris. Nathan became his greatest support but Simon remained a crumpled, humiliated, shattered man for the rest of his life. He, and they, never mentioned Mary Ellen, and they never let the name Maurice cross their lips. The child's mother had everything she asked for including a decree nisi. Well, what else would you expect when it came to Mary Ellen?

11

Now I prefer a pint and a pipe of St Bruno

The name Walter is of Old German origin, and its meaning is 'commander of the army'. Derived from the German 'walt', meaning 'rule', and 'heri', meaning 'army'.

His name went out of fashion,
Left behind for old men or used to ridicule:
'Where's Wally?' 'What a Wally!'
This Wally couldn't even command his dreams,
But he was steady, biddable, pliable.
Make of him what you will.

I thought, at first, it was a bit of fun, well, more than that perhaps, but it moved faster than I expected. I have no regrets, though to be honest I do feel like I did the dirty on Joe. Would that count as a regret? Mary doesn't do regret. Joe was alright really, boring, yes, out of his depth probably, but alright. She'll probably reach the same conclusion about me before long. I think I am different person when I am with her, but I remember Teresa Green soon got tired and gave up on me. Others did, too, one after the other. I think in reality I was, still am, a simple man. I work with my hands, I get paid a pittance, I like a pint, a pipe of St Bruno or even, at a pinch, Golden Virginia, an occasional tot of Johnny Walkers and steak and kidney pudding, with chips of course.

She made me different; she was feral, unpredictable, taunting, teasing. She drew me in and I thought she would spit me out when she had had enough. You wouldn't guess that now, looking at us. I'm still boring, smoking my pipe and eating the pie. Though now I have to sneak out for a pint, when she's not looking that is. She is rounder, old-lady plump, her face too lined to be covered by the slap she occasionally applies. It wasn't like that then. Those first few nights at the pub were electric. Suddenly, I felt I was the life and soul, I could make people laugh – make *her* laugh! It was a first for me. I couldn't help myself; I certainly couldn't think rationally and that was without the Boddingtons or Johnny Walkers. What do they call that female plant that swallows its prey – the flytrap something... is it Venus? It should be renamed the Mary Ellen Man-trap. I like that; that's just how it felt. A bit of lippy and a pair of pert boobs and I was caught, hopelessly stuck in the trap. And it has never let me go, though the boobs have sagged, the waistline expanded and I am more interested in the Boddingtons these days.

In the end, she led me, a sheep to the slaughter. I think I have messed up these metaphors, or used too many, but that just explains the hold she had (has) over me. My brain was everywhere, so was the rest of me, and in the end the rest of me won.

I followed instructions (or were they orders?) to the letter; it was easier that way. She never said it outright, but I presumed (I was too frightened to ask outright) that she was pregnant with *my* child. I was obliged. I scoured the streets of Gorton for some rooms to rent. Some rooms that I could afford to pay for with my pathetic council worker pay. In the end one of the lads knew of some lodgings in Peacock Street not far from the Billiard Hall. I didn't look properly, just agreed to the three rooms. It would mean that we could use one for Maurice and, if there was another on the way, him or her too, one for us and a sitting room. It was as good as I could get though I knew she would be aiming for more. She took over from there; she had done this before, she knew the patter. There was no question about the little lad, he was coming with us come hell or high water. I didn't mind, none of this was his mess and he was a funny little thing. He stood up to her, even then.

I think Joe knew the writing was on the wall. He had sensed the drifting away, more and more nights out on the town and all the rest. He was too weak to put up any fight, even if he had wanted to. She could have that effect if she wanted to, draining you of life till you begged her to stop. Sometimes I think it must have come as relief to him when she left. The spell was finally broken, the magic draining away fast down a sewer of humiliation. She spat him out the same way she had sucked him in, in one wretch of vomit. A warning to me of what might happen if I didn't toe the line or if, for her, something better came along. I never saw Joe again. Perhaps that was a good thing. I tried not to think about it, but it was hard with the little lad around staring at me with those deep black eyes and mop of thick black hair. She talked a lot about making a completely fresh start and Maurice was included.

'We'll call him Harold from now on,' she declared. 'Harold Miller. It has a nice, solid ring about it. And we can save the name Walter for the future', she continued with a wry, knowing smile that frightened me to death. Mrs Kemp, the landlady, never asked any questions. Pleased to have the little Miller family in her spare rooms, pleased with the rent too. Mary Ellen could make it all look so respectable.

We moved in and Mary never mentioned Joe or his family again. It was one of her 'no go' areas. As the years went by, she had a few of these but this one sealed her lips like the proverbial camel's arse in a sandstorm. I didn't push – why cause myself more grief?

*

For the next forty years, there were really only three occasions when Joe Daniels forced himself (or at least something about him forced itself) back into my consciousness. There was the day that Harold disappeared near Brook's Bar. The police dealt with that, but I suspected it was something to do with Joe. Then, some time after Walter had been born, in 1930, Mary Ellen decided we should get married. Fortunately, an eerie coincidence, early in 1931 Joe Daniels decided it was time to petition for a divorce. I suppose the two were linked but I had little to do with it other than being named on some legal document. By 1932, we were married and the now legitimate Miller family had two children, though Harold was not mine, of course. This was a fact never to be mentioned. Then, of course, there was the day of Harold's wedding. I expected it would all come out then but Mary Ellen kept an iron grip on any storytelling, and in the process I think she lost Harold. As always, I kept my counsel, hid in the shadows, weak as ever, and smoked another pipe of St Bruno.

Things had moved on in those seventeen or so years. I still worked for the Council; it was a steady job. We had left Mrs Kemp's rooms for a larger place not long after we had arrived. Mary Ellen had expectations she was determined to meet. Somehow, later, we managed to get one of the Victorian terraced houses on Heywood Street. It was a big bunion of a thing, like a warren with large rooms and an inside bathroom, though I remained committed to the outside khazi. I was never sure how we paid for it all but we did. I just took my pocket money for baccy and the odd beer. Apart from a few coppers in my pocket, that was all I needed and all I got. I know she made stuff, baby clothes, the odd dress. She was good with her hands like that, though she hated other household chores. I know she bought material from a warehouse back in Gorton or another in

Miles Platting but she would not go to the big one in Brook's Bar. She took in lodgers. Mrs Humbers, the preacher's widow, lived in the parlour, Tommy Rand, a lad from Styal orphanage, came and stayed for years. He had a room on the middle floor. My father, whom we called Papa, also had a bedroom on the that floor and the kids were in the attic. We had the room in the middle next to the back room and scullery. It seemed to work in its own way, as long as people kept in their place. Not just physically but in their place in the pecking order, the one Mary allotted them. Harold always rebelled – he stood up to her and she hated it. He was too strong to physically punish but she had other methods of torture. Sometimes for days no one was allowed to speak to the miscreant until he apologised. On other occasions, she would dock his pay or cut his food.

Mary started to lend money, for a little interest, of course. It started with the likes of Mrs Humbers, and other similar women on the street. Just a bob here and there to help them eke the week. She dealt with it all. 'Safe lending,' she called it, 'with a decent return.' She'd even charge family members a 'decent return' if they came cap-in-hand. She wrote all the details in a little book that she kept close or hidden in the dark bedroom Harold called her 'lair'. He, as always, was right, the only one brave enough to confront her, even to ignore her fainting dramatics. I was never too sure whether that was his father's spirit or whether he was built out of the same stuff as Mary Ellen. Perhaps that was why she doted on Walter, and stayed somewhat aloof from Harold. In Harold, she met her match, saw too much of herself to be comfortable. I liked having him around; it kept a check on some of her crueller manipulations. Sometimes, it provided more than a little amusement as I was sent scurrying for the smelling salts and she predictably fell back into her chair.

Harold was good for a pint at the Great Western. Most of all, we loved Vera, especially Papa. He adored her and their little girl Linda, too. Mind, Papa always had an eye for a pretty girl. Vera brought some lightness, some perfume into our musty home. And she learnt to stand her ground. It was inevitable that they would go, though apart from 'her indoors', we dreaded it. When it happened, we enjoyed the pantomime, like a rehearsed script with the wicked Widow Twanky to boot. Secretly, though, just like the pantomime we were on Cinders' and Prince Charming's side, silently cheering them on. The move to the council flat in Wythenshawe wasn't quite the prince's castle, but enough to get them away from the wicked Twanky.

I was going nowhere. Fully trained in service, and appropriately silent, I hung around the edges and took my chances for the odd pint. I was too old to play Buttons and never developed that spine that Harold had been given in his gene deposit – Ellis or Karavitch, it didn't matter. I knew where the smelling salts were kept, an early and necessary lesson. I could remove and put on shoes like a good prince, though I had ended up with an ugly sister, too fat to bend down herself. Fortunately, Vera and Harold didn't totally give up on us. She brought the kids to see us when she was visiting her mum on Talbot Street. I think it was out of duty but it was a highlight for Papa and me. Mary would use the kids to burrow her way back into Harold's family. My, she could pull off some remarkable stunts, usually around money, bribes and gifts used to disrupt and antagonise, to set one against the other. If we had time, I could tell you about the motor bike but it's water under the bridge, and that time she quickly realised she had gone beyond the pale. Harold had had enough and Vera, the lovely Vera, refused to let her tricks break up her home. Vera had a totally different way of handling her, a different more flexible spine, you might say, one that didn't break.

*

Young Walter got married but never had any kids – no surprise there. John, the youngest lad, had too many, bred like a rabbit. Walter was a surprising mix of his mother and me. At one point weak and at another manipulative. I never found him easy to love, not like Mary who thought the sun rose when he shit in the potty. John was a harder, more crass copy of Mary: light-fingered. No wonder he ended up inside Strangeways for a mercifully short stint. He was scheming, reckless but none too bright. I hope he wasn't like me at all. In a real way it was Harold I admired most, though of course he wasn't mine. I like to think he didn't hate me. His kids were refreshing. He had Linda, who lived with us at the beginning, and we watched her grow. She was all Shirley Temple ringlets mixed with Sugar Ray Robinson fists. Brian was made for stardom, James Dean style, though drink and the desire for the limelight would be his downfall. Geoff and Gary came later, much later. A kind of second wind. Gary had Harold's punch and cheek. With his curly mop of dark hair, he was fast and fearless. He was never too keen on his Fat Nana with horrible whiskers and he told her so. That's why he never liked Santa Claus – too much like his Nana in a silly red suit. Geoff always intrigued me. A scrawny thing, quiet and a bit bookish, but sharp.

The last time I saw them, I remember giving Geoff a little book I had kept in my room for years. I'm no book person, but this one had tickled me when I first saw it. The sketch on the front cover reminded me of my dad. *The Specialist* by Charles Sale was all about Lem Putt, a carpenter by trade who specialised in sanitary engineering – he built privvies. I saw Geoff's eyes light up as he held the gift and watched him smiling as he read the cover. Mary had wanted Geoff to be called Walter but he was no Wally. He'll be okay, I thought to myself, might not be a fighter like his dad, but he has his dad's wicked sense of humour.

12

It's a long way to 'Eureka'

The family name 'Karavitch': the meaning of this name is not listed.

Repeat ad nauseum, ad nauseum,
ad nauseum
'The meaning of this name is not listed'.
It can be changed: Corravitch, Karavitchev, Karawidz
even Kaye.
Someone said it meant 'hope', wouldn't that be good?
But who said it, when, why? Who knows?
No one knows!
Shame, but one can hope anyway!
Perhaps it was the same person that
said you could find anything on the internet?
They were wrong.

Geoff had two breakthrough moments in his 'roots research'. The first proved to be something of a red herring. Though later he concluded that if it wasn't for that cul-de-sac, he would probably not have persisted to his second enlightenment. It was all quite simple and obvious really.

Here's the first naivete:

He found he could easily access Mary Ellen and Joe's marriage certificate. Easy if you paid the fee, of course, which he did. As a vicar, he had written out hundreds of marriage certificates over the years, though he reflected that it was no longer part of the role and had been handed over to the Local Registrar. But during his ministry filling in those long, landscape green registers had been very much part of the ritual of Saturday morning tasks. Officially, they were not supposed to be written until the couple had made their vows but in practice, like all clergy, he used to take a chance and write them on the wedding day, but before the ceremony began. They were simple enough, but because they were a legal document, and you had to use blue/black permanent registrar's ink, he had never got overconfident when filling them in. Over-confidence led to not taking enough care and you could easily make a mistake, though most mistakes could be corrected. He hated making a correction for all posterity to see, putting his initials in the margin when he had crossed out part of an entry. He was proud of his registers, scooting them off to the vestry safe the minute the photographs had been taken. He lived in fear, as taught by his training incumbent, of a spilt bottle of ink on the white wedding dress to be sure, but worse a blot on the registers. They contained the minimum of information, names and ages of the couple, addresses and jobs. The witnesses' signatures, and then, if the couple agreed, and they usually did without question, father's names and status (jobs). Once or twice, Geoff had been a little slapdash but never on purpose. He remembered on one occasion when he came to make his quarterly return to the Registrar he couldn't read the signatures of the witnesses. He quickly did an indistinct squiggle on the return copy and sent it off, hoping it would suffice. Unfortunately, the Registrar wrote back, wanting a second copy and sending him a clean form back asking him to complete it. How would he remember the squiggles that his ignorance had produced in his last return? With a flourish, he dipped his pen in the ink and waved it in the right spot on the form. He had no idea how it could be read or whether it was anything like his last attempt. He licked the envelope and sent it off to the Registrar, hoping it would do the business. He never heard anything back, thank God. From then on, he always copied the witness signatures in pencil in the Register for later reference. He was a quick learner – not!

A more embarrassing moment was when, during a wedding ceremony, as he handed the groom the ancient fountain pen, he said to the groom: 'Put your weight on when you write!' meaning that the ink pen was a little temperamental and scratchy and needed a firm hand. He looked away for a moment, and then back again to see the groom had written John Smith, 12st 8oz. It was a margin correction to be embarrassed about and hopefully lost in the pages. One day he would have liked to do a search of all the marginal notes in the old books to see what other howlers he could turn up.

But don't get him started on funny wedding stories or you will never get him stopped. 'Do you remember the one where the bride…' 'Stop now! Right now, Miller!' he could hear his wife's order echo in his inner ear.

He knew, of course, that the records were useful for more than proof of a marriage. The little information they contained was a fascinating historical record of who married whom, what jobs they had, where they came from. He also knew that behind each record was a more intimate (and usually more interesting) human story: perhaps a secret romance or a loveless expected duty, even a marriage of convenience. But a story, nevertheless. And apart from the few recorded, simple facts they were often stories still to be told or that had been lost in the past. Certainly, behind Mary Ellen and Joe's certificate details there was Geoff's own story, his personal hinterland. He opened the brown envelope to see what secrets the certificate would reveal. Perhaps you have already guessed the answer. None! Well, almost none. There were a few facts he could follow up but there was also a nuisance of a problem that provoked in him a certain guilt. He could hardly read the looping scrawl of the elaborate cursive writing. Of course, he knew some of the names already but the ones he was really hoping to find, namely Joe's dad, were almost impossible to make out. The witnesses, too, had indecipherable names. He never for a minute thought that years from now some frustrated family member might be desperately trying to decipher his school-taught Nelson script in order to explore a family story, but they probably would. He hoped they would be more forgiving towards him than he, at the moment, felt for G. H Ramsbottom, Registrar in Manchester in 1925.

He decided not to give up yet and looked up the records that bore Mary Ellen's second marriage, much later in 1935, to Walter Miller, the man Hal always presumed was his dad and who Geoff knew as quiet, pipe-smoking 'Pa'. These lists only provided the names of the couples married that quarter. He found lurking at the top of a page, there in the margin, a correction, or, in this case, an addition. It was his first piece of usable evidence. It set his mind moving forward, ten to the dozen. 'Eureka!' he almost cried aloud. The marriage in 1935 of Walter Miller and Mary Ellen Daniels/Karavitch. As if out of the blue the 'Karavitch' name appears as an alternative to Daniels. So now the question that had been pursued morphed into: Who is Joe Daniels/Karavitch?

Geoff was on a roll and, as always, he worked solidly. He put his blinkers on, pushed ahead not totally without thinking but certainly without measured care. It took him no time at all to run down the rabbit hole. He was an expert genealogist after all – not! Now to find a Joe Karavitch in Manchester in 1925. He fed in the data and waited and watched the screen in anticipation. The records threw up a Karavitch family in South Manchester without any hesitation, procrastination or deviation. *Alleluia*! He had solved the riddle. Woolf and Dora Karavitch had moved to Manchester from Belfast in the late 1800s. They had moved from Russia to Dublin, then to

Belfast from Dublin and finally to Manchester. They were tailors, 'people of the scissors and ironing board' chasing work in the rag trade, and Manchester was supposedly a good place for materials, cotton and cloth workers.

Geoff moved fast now, digging deeper, searching beyond the basic records. He found a web site that connected with the Jewish Genealogical Society of Ireland (division of the Irish Jewish Museum) and a contact address. He sent off an enquiry and very quickly received a courteous and helpful response. It had taken so long to get anywhere in his research but now he was on a roller coaster, the riddle all but solved. Or was it? He was soon to learn that too much haste can produce a lot of waste – measured in time and dashed hopes!

The Irish researcher was incredibly helpful, meticulous in detail and probably a bit tickled to have a Christian priest (a Dean, no less) contacting him, exploring his so far unknown Jewish roots. Geoff got the feeling that he loved a problem to be solved and was addicted to such riddles. Firstly, he confirmed what Geoff had already unearthed. All very helpful and positive. He quickly found the Karavitch family of Dublin, Belfast and Manchester. Geoff could smell the end of the search like a spicy Russian goulash!

Woolf and Annie Karavitch arrived in Dublin in the late 1800s. They were one couple among many who had escaped the latest pogrom in Russia following the assassination of Tsar Alexander II, which was blamed on the Jews. Many were hoping to get to America, as were many Irish would-be emigrants at the time. They had brought Annie's mother and sister along with them or maybe they followed later, after they had settled. Woolf was born in Russia in 1870 and his wife, Annie Barnett, a few years later in 1876. Woolf was a tailor and, most probably like the other Jews who settled in Dublin, came from a *shtetel* close to Kovno in the old Russian empire. After the Second World War, Kovno was renamed Kaunas, the second city of present-day Lithuania. The exciting bit, the bit that would lead Geoff, hopefully, to Joe Daniels was that Woolf and his family moved first to Belfast and then to Manchester – South Manchester, too. It was easy to trace their moves as they followed work available for a tailoring family. Manchester was in the end a good fit with a lively rag trade and the evidence is that Woolf did well. By 1911, Woolf had his own business and the family had a live-in servant. They also had, in the 1911 census return, four children, one girl and three lads. Could one of these three lads be Joe Daniels? At this point, Geoff's imagination carried him away; far-off lands, dangerous escapades, risk-taking journeys. Was this the stuff of books and films? *Fiddler on the Roof* and *The Sound of Music* sprang to mind. But there was little evidence he could unearth exceptional musical skills or dangerous chases across mountain borders. That's the problem with census data. It gives data – simple facts, and even they are not always correct, sometimes they can't even be read; remember the vicar's pretentious handwriting on the marriage certificate!

Geoff was learning about amateur genealogy research the hard way. It was always too easy to assume stuff, that what you read was true. Even with that in mind, you could build a picture of facts, simple data, but found yourself no nearer answering the more intriguing questions about lives lived. And when it came to names, people were annoyingly inconsistent, even sometimes deceitful. Plus, there were, as you might expect, lots of people with the same name. All this fuelled Geoff's overactive story-telling brain. He remembered for instance when he received an email that was really sent to another Geoff Miller but on the same cloud server. At first sight, it was quite juicy. Some rich namesake seemed to be having an illicit, and rather racy, liaison with an international work colleague – or so Geoff's over-active imagination dreamt up. Without stopping to think, he replied to the sender (in his mind a beautiful, power-suited executive straight from *Suits* or *Dynasty*). 'Sorry, your email has arrived in the wrong inbox. I am Geoff Miller, a priest in the UK. Your liaison sounds risky. Hope you are enjoying it!' He never got a reply. Only afterwards did he stop his impetuous and compulsive dreaming and wonder whether he had totally misread the situation – it was none of his business after all. He hoped it at least gave them a laugh and whatever was happening (it could have been an attempt to keep a long-distance relationship alive), they felt just a little bit naughty.

More seriously, in his early research, he also unearthed a Walter and Mary Ellen Miller getting married in the same year as his grandparents in the USA and, believe it or not, having a first child that they named Harold. Following that up might have led Geoff down a deeper rabbit hole. He learnt that most names, even with connected dates, are not unique or that unusual!!

But back to the mysteriously named Woolf Karavitch – not that mysterious or unusual in Germanic countries – but certainly different to the British ear. Geoff pondered Woolf's family and their settling in Ireland, and then Manchester, with keen interest. The kindly man at the Irish Jewish research centre explained that their journey was not that unusual. Persecution, war and poverty were big drivers for emigrants from the Baltic countries at the end of the nineteenth century. So was the move from Dublin to Belfast to Manchester. They were simply following opportunities for work, as the Industrial Revolution took hold and Manchester became an international centre for the rag trade. Tailors galore moved in that direction and some became hugely rich and famous: check out Marks & Spencer, Burtons, Moss Brothers and Ben Sherman for starters. Sadly, there were no Karavitches among them. Geoff smelled the end of his search but his nose for the truth was failing him.

Anyway, back to Woolf and Annie Karavitch who left the old Russian Empire and headed for the UK in the 1880s. Their first child, Abraham, was born in Belfast, then there was a girl Doris, followed by Jacob (Jack), and finally Norman. In 1911, we find the family settled in 96 Moss Lane West in Manchester. While Woolf worked as a tailor, the others worked in shops and businesses or were still infants. Geoff thought it all seemed to fit together, the final pieces of the jigsaw. But which one was Joe Daniels? The obvious contenders had to be Abraham or Jacob, though why they decided to take the name Joe Daniels remained a mystery. Geoff had learnt that dates could easily be misrepresented, just as names could easily morph.

The first, perhaps, by human error, the latter for a whole variety of reasons. There was plenty of evidence of name-changing in Woolf's family, from the obvious misspelling of Woolf, then he found Jacob, known as Jack, and Norman Karavitch who later became known as Norman Kaye, the last name announced in the London Evening Standard in 1949. Some of these changes were simply in the transliteration from Russian, Lithuanian or Yiddish, others were attempts at Anglicised names that helped Jewish folk melt into the background. Even more, sometimes a new name was chosen to signal a fresh start. All understandable, but not too helpful for the family historian. He was learning that it was even more confusing for Jewish families who also all bore Jewish names, or Hebrew names, so that could be quite difficult in identifying individuals or on occasions could be the exact opposite and better help identify someone. It seemed like some of those emigrating from Russia were keen for completely fresh starts, new names and new identities. Maybe that was true of one of Woolf's sons. However, there was an immediate problem with any link to the Joe Daniels' story. A simple difficulty. Even if he used a false name, which one of Woolf's sons could have been Joe? Abraham, Jacob or even young Norman? They were all born in the wrong years, all had other wives and families, too. This would have been deception on a grand scale. They didn't seem like liars and bigamists, though what do liars and bigamists look like when you only have their signatures and addresses to go on? Geoff wavered in whether he should even dare to dig deeper, some skeletons should be allowed to remain in the cupboard. There they could rot and disintegrate into indistinguishable dust. In the meantime, he had reached the conclusion he was in a cul-de-sac. Perhaps he should leave it there and get back to being retired! But guess what? The niggling curiosity did not fail him, and besides, he had little else to do. At least that's what his wife said.

*

'He's behind you!' they shouted until they were hoarse. They bellowed in his ears from every annoying direction. He had never much liked pantomimes and suffered this one with quiet, miserable protest. He didn't want to be the party pooper, not again. Pantomimes, he thought, were an odd mixture of gender-bending slapstick. Which he had no real objection to, except he found it boring, crass, childish and it definitely didn't tickle his inner child. He hated the jokes:

'What did the mouse buy at the music shop?'

A mouse-organ!

'Do you know her?'

Yes, it was our Monica!'

'What goes: ha, ha plonk?'

A man laughing his head off!

The rest were usually about farts or burps or a just a custard pie shoved in someone's face. At least that gave the thrower some pleasure. Personally, he would like to 'Stop it, Geoff!!' he corrected himself.

He continued to suffer quietly, hoping he wouldn't spoil the fun. 'He's behind you!' they roared, yet still Buttons (stupid, sad Buttons) failed to cotton on. For some reason the obviousness of it all struck him hard. Without obvious rhyme or reason, he called to mind a Roald Dahl story he had read to his school class over forty years ago, when he was a teacher. The brain is a strange contraption, working so often mysteriously, making weird connections in dream-like sequences. At least his did. Anyway, the memory amused him more than the panto. The story was from a collection called *Tales of the Unexpected*. He remembered the gist of it and especially the final line. A pregnant woman had found out her husband was cheating on her. She waited until he came home from the office. Sat him down with a G&T and then, from behind, hit him on the head with a frozen leg of lamb. She immediately put the meat in the oven to cook. Went out and came back again to 'discover' her murdered husband. She called the police. They came with a whole forensic team in tow, including a kind WPC to comfort her in her terrible distress. The lamb was by now roasted crispy so she got it from the oven. She was numb in shock, so, as a distraction in her distress, she served the police team roast lamb sandwiches. They were frantically searching for a murder weapon but without success. 'Bet it's right under our nose,' said the detective as he took another bite of his fresh meat sandwich.

A pantomime clown not clocking what was behind him in open view, a detective chewing on a roast lamb sandwich while looking for a murder weapon ... what was happening to him? Old age was certainly kicking in – and fast. His memory was making weird links.

'Boo, boo... boo!' the kids annoyingly hollered, interrupting his thinking. Then a light bulb switched on in his head, and he wanted to cheer. Random electrical pathways throughout his brain connected like a telephone exchange being plugged in or a web search engine bringing conclusions to a complicated request. Now he wanted to join the panto chants and cheers.

This Joe Daniels stuff ... perhaps he was not seeing what was right under his nose, in plain sight, so to speak? Perhaps he was getting bogged down with names and dates and fantasies and just not seeing the obvious. Funny how that works: when you lose something in the house and you search everywhere. Under papers, cushions, down the side of the settee, even in his case, in the fridge – he had found his car keys there once. Then your partner comes in and sees your frantic confusion and says, 'Is it these keys you are looking for, the ones on top of the kitchen workbench?' You want to shout, 'But I have looked there, more than once too.' Sometimes you look but don't see. That's the whole point of those air-tag things he had got for Christmas last year. You attach them to your keys and they are traceable through your phone, his wife told him. That's what memories need, he decided, or the whole brain needed in Geoff's case. Perhaps that what pantomimes are: memory tags, logic jogs. They basically annoy you so much you have to think about other things. They caused a memory jolt. He liked that thought and he smiled to himself as he applauded the end of the first act.

As he ate the ice-cream and settled down for Act Two (just

another 45 minutes, thank God), he remembered a clever book he had read some years ago – see, the memory tag was still working. Thomas Kuhn, a classic. It was called *The Structure of Scientific Revolutions*, or something like that. Just what you need when you are watching the ugly sisters trying to force a pair of glass slippers on their huge bunioned feet. Geoff was no scientist but what he remembered was that Kuhn found that most scientists don't look at the evidence to make a theory. Instead, they have a theory and try and make the evidence fit. Most revolutionary science is almost 'discovery by accident'. Perhaps the greatest example is Fleming finding penicillin in the discarded petri dish. In other words, even scientists can miss what is right under their noses. Was that what he had been doing with Woolf Karavitch and his family? Was he missing something right under his nose? The link that would end the search for Joe Daniels – was it in plain sight? Well, if so, according to Kuhn, perhaps he was in good company!

As the final curtain came down and the cast took another bow, he could have spit when they had to deliver their prepared encore piece. He decided now wasn't the time to shout, 'Boo!'. He wanted to get back to his research. Still, he could not deny that this production had been of real value to him. Tonight, he would raise a glass to Cinders and start his search again. This time looking for the 'bleedin' obvious'.

So, to the second naivete:

The enlightenment? With thanks to Cinders and her ugly sisters. Geoff hoicked all his papers out again and switched on the computer. He slowly poured over the data, flicking aimlessly through the papers, and scrawled his saved web sites. He didn't know what he was looking for, just hoping there might be a magical connection. The only link between Joe Daniels and the name Karavitch was on the record of Mary-Ellen's second marriage. It seemed to appear left field, or out of the blue. It was that tenuous link that had led him to Woolf, Annie and their sons, none of whom had been even born in the right year, never mind bore a name similar to Joe. He had then got carried away with Dublin, Belfast and Manchester; with *shtetls* in Russia, and now Lithuania. He had learnt on the way that names could always be very fluid, especially among immigrants desiring a fresh start, even more so among minority groups like Jews, wanting to hide or be assimilated in their new homes. New names signalled new identities, new possibilities, the shaking off of the past. But they didn't make family research easy! He wondered how much a new name helped people create new identities or shed old cultures. In his experience, identity was bound up in names. It was hard to imagine someone you knew well with a different name. Perhaps that was the point. He knew himself that names evoked certain feelings and responses. Call him Geoffrey, and he was a little boy in trouble at school. Call him Geoff, and he was a pal. Perhaps those who changed their names wanted to become a completely new person. He'd met that with people transitioning from one sex identity to another. Often they chose names that didn't fit into straightforward gender categories: Willow, Ashleigh, Zar, Rain... They were refusing to be defined, perhaps still searching for their inner selves. So why choose Joe Daniels if your name was Karavitch? Just a name you liked or admired? Or maybe trying to hide from a past rather than to build a future? He'd been through these arguments so many times without even the glimmer of a resolution. Probably, an unsolvable mystery, but could he even locate this Joe? Could he find him in the records? He certainly hadn't had much luck so far, not a birth or a census entry or a death. Just a mention in a marriage. So, he was left with the fact that the only connection to Karavitch was a reference on Mary Ellen's second marriage certificate. What he had never considered was the obvious fact that to make a second marriage, she had be widowed or divorced. No death of a Joe Daniels was recorded, so her second marriage implied she was divorced. That was highly unusual for a woman in 1935 but nevertheless, that's what she was. The light bulb in his brain flickered! Could he access divorce records? He had never thought of that. Such records could be scanty in this period, though they did exist. However, they were not available on the standard ancestry sites. This was the second naivete, the hiding in full sight. He could easily access the divorce papers that did exist at the National Archive, at Kew in London. He found the enquiry form and filled it in online and waited. Why had he never thought of this before? Too busy looking at Joe Daniels' records meant he failed to look a bit further ahead. It wasn't marriage details he needed; it was exactly the opposite: divorce records.

And BINGO!

Details came back relatively quickly and without any cost. The puzzle was solved as simply and as easy as that. In 1931, the husband of Mary Ellen Ellis filed for divorce, naming Walter Miller as the co-respondent. The name of the husband was *Simon Israel Karavitch, otherwise known as Joe Daniels*. Now, Geoff was like a child at the pantomime. The fairy godmother had waved her wand, Buttons had graduated. Slap your leg – cheer!

He was able to find Simon Israel quite easily; indeed, without any difficulty. It was a different branch of Karavitches, but maybe a related one. Simon Israel (sometimes Solomon) was the second son and third child of Harris (also Hirsch) and Rose (also Rosa and Rhoda) of Berkley Street in Salford in the 1901 Census. He followed Simon a little. Initially, he was listed in census returns as an errand boy aged 16, later a tailor like his father, much later he lived with his brother Nathan, still in Manchester. He was listed as divorced when he lived with Nathan in the census of 1941, so he had not remarried, and by then he worked as a fish and fruit salesman in Nathan's shop. Nathan seemed to use the surname Kaye, and other Karavitches liked that anglicised name. There is no reference to Simon even adopting another alias or re-using his Joe Daniels nomenclature. Perhaps, Joe did disappear with the disintegration of his marriage to Mary Ellen. Maybe he just decided to live a quiet life, any dreams of excitement over and done with; once bitten, twice shy! Possibly, he had had enough of any limelight and felt shamed by his failure, so just kept his head down. We will never know. But what about Maurice? Did Simon stay in touch or even try to? Geoff remembered his dad's strange recall of the police chase and being returned to Mary Ellen's flabby clutches. Simon must have tried and failed, and was well and truly warned off. Meanwhile, Mary Ellen had rebuilt another life with Walter Miller whom she married in 1932. She had given birth to two further children: Walter junior born in 1930 before her marriage to Walter, his father, and then John in 1934. Her marriage to Joe lasted no more than a few years and by the time she was divorced, she had already had another child to Walter Miller. It was Simon who filed for the divorce and it was no doubt granted on the admission of adultery. This brought an end to one chapter of Mary Ellen's history – one which she refused to talk about. She wanted it buried. Did she feel shame, sadness, regret? Were they some of the building bricks with which she built her self-protection? Whatever, Mary Ellen was a feisty woman long before she was known to Geoff as Nana: the wicked grandma!

13

Maurice or Harold: same difference!

The name Maurice is derived from the Latin name Mauritius, which means 'dark-skinned' or 'Moorish'. Its etymological roots can symbolise diversity, strength and resilience.

The name Harold derives from the Old English *name* Hereweald, derived from the elements 'here' meaning 'army', and 'weald' meaning ' powerful, mighty'. It was the name of the last Anglo-Saxon king of England before the Norman conquest, and a name that's long been associated with a pipe-smoking, bespectacled grandpa or uncle.

Here's one in the eye for you, Hal.

You may think you are strong

but now you have to bounce back.

Now you will put your strength and your power to the test.

It's not enough to strut and stagger

But remember

you are who you are, not what you are called.

We left Harold Miller, aka Maurice Daniels, at the altar in St Margaret's Church on Whalley Road. Well, not quite. To be more exact, he was in the musty old vestry with the lily-livered parson, both pouring over the landscape, pale-green marriage registers. His young bride was just arriving at the west door, blooming in more ways than one. He was seventeen, a cocky, strutting seventeen, but in love. His arrival in church and his venturing into that vestry had left him dumbstruck. He could cope with a left-hook anytime but this was well and truly below the belt, timed for maximum damage. If he was honest, he was having difficulty in processing this new information. He wasn't that surprised that his mother was still playing her games but he had to admit that he never saw this coming. How could he have lived all these years in complete ignorance? How could she let him live a lie? This Maurice Daniels name – how could it be his? But it was, and before his very eyes it was, written in three different registers in that blue/black permanent registrar's ink. He played it over again in his head and could make no sense of it. The name didn't fit him, it was alien, like talking about someone else. He had questioned many things but always questioned them as Harold Miller. Now they were suggesting, no he was being *told*, that he was someone else, someone he didn't know. And his father: Who was Joe Daniels? Did it matter?

Something somewhere, thank God, was urging him to act differently. This wasn't going to be resolved with fisticuffs, his preferred method. Today of all days more important things were at stake. More important people were waiting for him. She was heading up the aisle. A pretty girl, whom he loved, a foetus growing apace in her womb. His baby. It took all his restraint not to rush to Heywood Street and shake the truth out of the old witch, but, like a magnet, instead he was drawn to the altar and to Vee.

He couldn't hide his anger and bewilderment, his dark eyes full of raw rage, but as he held Vee's hands she calmed him so easily, so gently. He would sort this out later. Now he stared at her eyes, which entranced him with their greenish-brown hue. One eye was darker than the other – he hadn't noticed that before. There was lots he hadn't noticed before. But there was time yet. So far, he had rarely assessed, or readily examined, his life. He had worked on impulses, drives, urges. Only now did he notice the tempest inside him. Vee saw it; she liked it because she alone could tame it.

Hal's earliest years were a blur. School was a wash-out, to say the least. He remembered more readily the cigarettes he got from the street vending machines. The Saturday morning fights in the back-alleyways, all for money. To make a challenge, you placed a small plank on your shoulder and the would-be opponent would knock it off. Then it began. No rules except street rules. Fists, no kicking, give up if one of them was out for the count, or ceded the fight. Hal was scrawny, but rampant; he took opponents by surprise. He had a good motto: *If there's nothing else, then go for the kneecaps,* and it usually worked.

'Always remember,' he told his own lads later. 'Make sure there is one of them in a hospital bed as well as you!'

Fortunately, his sons didn't always follow his advice or his ways. As his eldest son once informed him, 'Dad, when you are small, it's better to be intelligent ... and fast.'

Hal, however, preferred the fist to sort things out and it was only Proctor's Lads' Club that could mould his raw energy and stubbornness into an asset. He had fallen into labouring work when he was just a lad. Living at his Aunt Sara-Anne's in Denby Dale, Yorkshire, he was the first in the mine. He was fourteen, and it was hard work in every way, but he liked it. He certainly preferred it to Claremont Road School and Mr 'Strap-happy' Higgins. After his time down the pit, he picked up labouring work back home in Manchester, where he worked for a while on the new Barton Bridge built over the canal. Then he had something of a brainwave; he was no fool. Was it his itchy feet or a spirit of entrepreneurism? Maybe they are both related ... Anyway, he decided he wanted his own business. He got hold of a ladder and a couple shammy leathers and he started a window cleaning round. It worked. In no time he was whistling around the streets picking up new customers. The cheeky, cocky Miller lad would do your windows for a bob or two. He had a mate from Proctor's Gym who shared the round, Fred Burns, who they called 'Fatty Burns' for obvious reasons. Fat or not, he could go at some speed up and down those bloody ladders. They had their pit-stops all worked out: Mrs Battersby on Raven Street was good for a cup of tea and a change of water; Ethel Ramsden on Coronation Street would do the same with some cake thrown in, if you timed it right; best to avoid Mrs Ardent as she lived up to her name in that negligee – good for a laugh and a tale at the pub but a frightening sight before lunch; however, it was the MacKnights on Talbot Road he liked best of all. Old Ma Mac was sweet, when she wasn't drunk, and Vee, the youngest girl, was a real peach. Later, after he was married to the peach, he would branch out into chimney sweeping. He got all the proper stuff, no half-measures, such as his large, spiked, round flat brushes at the end of the ever-expanding canes that he learnt to screw on as he twisted the brush up the chimney. He learnt how to gauge the routes and crannies that each chimney had; indeed, he was a master at it, though it took some strength to hold the brush taut and not let it spin out of control. It was like he was back in the pit at Denby, shifting those carts from track to track.

When he was about fifteen, he progressed from the bare-fist fighting in the back alley to Proctor's Gym on Silver Street. He began going on a Saturday morning when for sixpence a go you could spar in the ring with one of the future champs in training. Soon he was training alongside them. He started in the bantamweight category but as he got older and filled out a bit, he moved into the featherweight group, all 127 pounds of him. He could throw a good punch but most of all he was fearless and soaked up pain. Later, with his brother-in-Law, Tommy Taylor (Vee's sister, Ethel's, husband) they did a few amateur fights. They were good drinking pals. Tommy was as big as Hal was small; he could carry Hal over his shoulder when he'd had too much in the pub. But sometimes he gave up and forgot where he had left him. More than once, Hal had been ditched in a hedge and left until the morning. They shared a bout once at the Free Trade Hall and it could have been the launch of a boxing career. It wasn't. Just as Hal was about to go in the ring, this bloke cornered him.

'Throw it, lad, throw the fight. We'll see you all right.'

Hal was flustered and unsure what to do. Tommy was in the corner and he said to do as they said, it wasn't worth the grief. So, he did, and he was punished by his pathetic opponent. The lad went feral and all Hal did was hold back. Hal was battered but more than that he was humiliated. Never again. It wasn't worth the wad of notes passed his way. He kept his promise to himself: *Never again!* Let some other punch-drunk wannabee take the pain.

Now here he was, at the altar in St Margaret's Church taking a step he never expected so soon…'For better, for worse, for richer, for poorer, in sickness and in health.' The words washed over him, soothed him. Vee squeezed his hand and looked into his eyes. She was vulnerable, fragile, but strong and beautiful. She was his Vee, so bugger Mary Ellen. He would deal with that old witch later.

They arrived back at Heywood Street as Mr and Mrs Miller (or was it Daniels?). He'd kept his cool, but now he wanted to make a real plan. He asked his ma gently about the name.

'Who was Joe Daniels?' he quizzed.

Cue the deep sigh, the call for salts, the fabulous histrionics as she sank back into her corner chair.

'Leave it, lad,' pleaded Pa, spineless as ever. 'Don't spoil the day. Let's take your bride down to the Great Western and down a few pints.'

With that, the matter was closed, until later when Mary Ellen was her usual tight arsed self. And she had a big arse.

Mary Ellen and Pa thought it was over, that they could carry on as before and Hal let them think that. Walter (the younger one) thought that too; he was a weak mammy's lap lad. A nancy boy who couldn't box his own shadow. He flounced around, trying to please the old witch, and she slavered after him. It sickened Hal to watch him in action. With Vee by his side, he would bide his time, wait to pounce. It was a new art for him but not that different from a good boxing bout. Look for the weak points, keep moving, find the unguarded moves: defend, block and, when you were sure, when the opportunity arrived, go hell for leather, hit direct for maximum damage with every bit of power you could muster.

Assured she had put everything back in its tidy box, Mary Ellen carried on playing her games. She relaxed again, crisis over. Looking back, Hal realised she didn't always plan or scheme, she simply did what came naturally. She was hard-wired that way. Inch by inch, she encroached on his business, offering to balance the books at first, then taking them over. Soon, Fatty Burns had moved on and she started weak Wally Walter on the rounds, as some supposed help. It felt like Hal was working for her. Patience Hal, patience lad: your time will come.

Of course, he had never heard of *Simchat Torah*, never heard of the Pale, but he knew he needed a fresh start; it was his time for an ending and a beginning. A time to move out and move on, into an uncharted landscape. He had never felt the need to escape before but now he felt trapped and he couldn't catch his breath. History repeats itself, they say, but he didn't know just how true that was. Perhaps he never would.

For Hal and Vee, *Goldene Medina* proved to be not more than a bus ride away. Wythenshawe! A huge housing estate on the edge of Manchester. Houses upon houses built on farmland and threatened every ten minutes by low-flying noisy aircraft. The planes were an advantage for Hal and Vee in that they frightened Mary Ellen so much that she ducked every time one flew over their flat. The time that one crashed into the roof of a house on Shadow Moss Road heightened her fear. It was probably the only good thing to come out of such a horrible tragedy. Though they were just a bus ride away (the 101 or 106, which stopped outside the Great Western), she didn't like to visit them. Thank God!

For once Hal had a steady job, on the buses. He loved it: the uniform, the shifts, the daily craic. Sometimes the craic got him in trouble. Not everyone appreciated him shouting, 'The dead centre of Manchester,' as they approached Southern Cemetery. He never much liked that cemetery all his life, claiming it was too near to Withington Hospital when he was an in-patient. He had a point; this huge burial ground (the largest in the UK and the second largest in Europe) was probably built next to the old Chorlton Union Workhouse (which became the hospital) on purpose, or vice versa. Hal looked forward to taking his driving test and becoming (*Da da!*) a bus driver! Though this was, in fact, never to be as he had his first epileptic fit just a few days before and lost the lot. No one wanted to take on a risk like that, not even Manchester Bus Corporation. It was another broken dream alongside his life-long dream to own a newsagent shop. Hal liked selling things, handling the goods doing the deal, and especially counting the cash. It would have been a good investment except for stocks of cigarettes which, in his hands, would probably have gone up in smoke, in particular the Capstan Full Strength which he had smoked since he was twelve, buying two fags with two matches in a little pack from the vending machine. Later, he would get through forty a day. He didn't much care for filters, spending a few hours cutting them off each cigarette when he had been given a duty-free box by someone returning from a holiday in Spain. He was a bit like that with new fandangle stuff. Scissors and teabags (and lettuce and freezers) come quickly to mind.

But he, along with Vee and the kids, were as happy as they could be in Wythenshawe. After the flat, they got a house in Peel Hall and there he settled for the rest of his life. Even without work, he had Vee and the kids. He did wrestle with not being able to work, often venturing a shift at the bakery, though that would, after a few days, knock him back and he would take to his bed. Other than that, he never ventured far, but unlike Vee he never wanted to. He never left England, not even to nearby Wales. He said he didn't care much for the Welsh. If he had found out that his maternal grandparents were both from Pontypridd, he might have made an even earlier grave. Probably from laughing too much – at himself. It wasn't unheard of, dying of laughing that is. 'What a way to go!' he would declare. His boxing-cum-drinking pal, Tommy Taylor (Vee's brother-in-law) died laughing at Tommy Cooper one night. Hal preferred Harry

Worth but both comedians annoyed Vee. He did like Southport, though he was never sure why. After Vee died, it was the only journey he could be persuaded to take other than to visit Geoff in the North East. Linda and family took him to the Pontin's Holiday Camp. Bizarrely, he liked the dodgems, loved the one-armed bandits and suffered the singer in the loosely called 'Cocktail Lounge', though with the latter he got fed up of the same routine every night.

'If he sings that one about a blanket on the floor again, I'll personally shove it up his...'

'Dad shush, stop it!' the puritanical Geoff declared when he visited them for a few days.

The holiday camp (once voted the worst holiday centre in the UK and often dubbed HMP Southport) was like a run-down council estate by the sea but at least it brought a smile to his face when not much else would.

Looking back over his life, he faced some real challenges. No wonder he was such a tough cookie; he had to be. Out of work in his thirties with no real prospects, dogged by ill-health, he took solace in Diazepam and sleeping pills. In his early fifties, a stroke left him struggling down one side. He mellowed as the years went by, and perhaps he more than mellowed. A stroke can play games with emotions and it certainly did with his.

'He'd get weepy at a Western,' Vee used to say. And he would, especially any starring John Wayne. Perhaps that was all a counterbalance to the face he presented in his early days or maybe this was who he was when his filters of self-preservation had been rumbled. It was Vee who could handle him better than anyone. She was the one who could empty the little yellow capsules of their toxic powder and replace it with sherbet, and still survive to tell the tale. She could calm him, laugh at (and with) him, and chide him with real effect. Perhaps it was simply because she could see through the veneer to his wisdom, his cares and ultimately his soft, mushy centre. She knew that his stoic face was simply bravado.

Hal would never have described himself as religious, far from it, perhaps the opposite. He liked his fags, he couldn't stop himself uttering expletives, was addicted to sarcastic and sometimes risqué jokes which more than occasionally got him into trouble. Religion was not for the likes of him, he would declare. It was a crutch for wimps, something good as the butt of the odd joke (said the actress to the bishop!), but not to be taken seriously in any way.

When Vee agreed to start the Girls' Brigade at the local church, he thought it was something to do with that whispered woman's condition, 'the Change'. It was yet another useful topic for teasing her (an addictive pastime), especially as the uniform reminded him of the Sally Army.

'All you need now is a tambourine,' he would rib as he shook a plate and sang Hallelujah.

But he couldn't refuse a challenge or a call for help. The challenge came from Vee who explained that there was going to be a darts competition between the Women's Fellowship and the Men's Society. They were looking for some men and women to make up the teams. He agreed; he liked darts. The call for help came from the young curate. First, it was getting the windows clean, then setting out the chairs in the mission hall that stood for a church on the estate. He soaked his shammy leathers and looked for some ladders to use. He was hooked. A darts match (which he won) and a shammy leather changed his life. He never became one of those 'born again Christians', but he found his place. A place where he was seen as wise, fun and the salt of the earth. It changed him, and Vee; in fact, all the family. So much so that when Brian returned on furlough from his RAF posting in Singapore, he hardly recognised them – not in looks, of course, but in how they had begun to live.

Much had stayed the same. Hal still never wore his teeth, and he still smoked and swore like a trooper, but he had settled. They were all much more settled. Brian never got over the fact that he was no longer the saviour with a bulging wallet. Perhaps in many ways Hal had found his niche or, more correctly, had a purpose, some meaning. It was this simple faith that got him through the next trials, the worse he could imagine. Vee took ill and quickly succumbed to an awful cancer. It was, he thought, the wrong way around. He should have gone first; she still had more to live for. He followed within a year.

There was still, however, one regret, one niggle that had always haunted him. That, try as he may, he had never solved the riddle of Joe Daniels. More importantly, he had never got to meet his real father properly. He hadn't received that fatherly approval that he had watched his own sons enjoy. What would Joe have made of him? Perhaps not much, at least in those middle years. But he would have liked to present Joe with Linda, Brian, Geoff and Gary. He was proud of them. And he couldn't for a minute imagine that Joe Daniels would not have fallen in love with Vee. He confessed just once that he had toyed with the idea of dropping the name Harold Miller and using the name Maurice Daniels. It would have been a costly thing to change his kids' names legally. What would have been achieved, though, other than perhaps a clean slate, a greater distance from Mary Ellen? She would still have been his mother and anyway by then she had lost her hold over him. She had moved out to the Darnhill Estate near Rochdale, to a small flat in a tower block. All part of the great Moss Side slum clearance of the sixties. Just her and Pa, a shadow of her former self, well, in power not weight. Her empire was diminished to a fifth-floor, one-bedroom flat and a balcony that she never went on. She didn't like heights. For Hal, saving that one regret about not ever knowing his real father, Joe Daniels, he was at last at home in his own skin. Surrounded by Vee and his family, he was at peace with himself.

14

Beyond the Pale

Pale: from Middle English 'pale', 'pal', borrowed from Old French 'pal', from Latin 'pālus' ('stake', 'prop'). English inherited the word 'pole' (or, rather, Old English 'pāl') from a much older Proto-Germanic borrowing of the same Latin word.

A post, a fence, a wall can make a prison,

mark a boundary, or protect a home.

Perhaps it depends which side of it you are on

or want to be on.

Beyond the pale can be freedom and opportunity

Or it might just be taking you too far.

The plane circled, and they caught the first glance of verdant fields, farms and the edge of a city landscape. Geoff thought to himself, 'This is doing things backwards.' It was a flight to retrace the steps that his great-grandfather had taken, a journey that had impacted his life. How strange was that? It wasn't a lone journey; others had wanted to join the trek. It had become a family affair, but this time, unlike for their ancestors, it was a visit *to* the Pale not an escape *from* it. To be sure, it was way more comfortable and less hazardous than the Wilson Shipping Line crossing made by Harris and Rose, in the opposite direction, so many years before. Though one could hardly call a budget airline seat luxurious.

Kaunas, now the second city of Lithuania, bustles as it continuously reinvents itself for each new era: temporary capital, economic and centre of learning, centre for Lithuanian national revival, UNESCO city of design, a World Heritage site, the European City of Culture. Kaunas has dominated this region for centuries, though for many of them it was known as Kovno. It has a strategic position at the congruence of two large rivers, the Neris and the Nemunas. Today, the red roofs of the old town are pierced with the steeples and towers of ancient churches, domed public buildings, and the infamous fort. The magnificent inter-war buildings have earned it a well-deserved World Heritage status.

When the Red Army occupied Vilnius in 1919, Kovno (Kaunas) became the temporary capital of Lithuania, a position it held until 1939. Russian and German control followed and then in came the Russians again – they're like that. However, on 16 February 1989, Cardinal Vincentas Sladkevičius for the first time called for the independence of Lithuania in his sermon at the Kaunas Cathedral. After the services, 200,000 people gathered in the centre of Kaunas to participate in the dedication of a new monument to freedom to replace the monument that had been torn down by the Soviet authorities after World War II. The rest is history... well, for now. However, there are Putin-shaped clouds on the horizon.

But Geoff and his fellow travellers are not tourists, they are not here to visit this exciting city, fascinating as it is. Not this time, anyway. They leave the airport and search – successfully, thank God – for their rental car. So begins an adventure navigating new roads and new towns. Eventually, crammed in the small car, they find the E67 and begin their first experience of Lithuanian roads. Fortunately, it takes little more than an hour and with need of little direction.

En route, they get their first glimpses of the Lazdijai region, dominated by blue lakes and the green shades of forestry. Excitement at the land's beauty is more than a little infused with the thrill of knowing that these are the forests, paths and villages where Harris and Rose, Woolf and Annie played and worked. Soon they would stand in the village where the Karavitches lived, worked and wed. It was from where they escaped a pogrom in 1888 and led them to 'Cottonopolis'. The rest is history – of a sort.

Today Rudamina is a small settlement of little more than two hundred and fifty inhabitants. It has never been that big, though it has seen times of prosperity. It once had a flourishing Jewish community, artisans, tailors, shoemakers, carpenters, makers of wooden tiles and harness makers. Some Jewish families farmed while others owned the brick and ceramic tile factory, the wool-combing plant and the distillery. In 1931, all the shops belonged to Jewish families. Its beautiful synagogue was a popular place of prayer for people form surrounding towns at festivals and celebrations. Sadly, none of this history is visible to the visitor today. The small, neat settlement of houses is dominated by an ancient hill fort and the large eighteenth-century white church of the Holy Trinity. Indeed, references to its former Jewish community are hard to find, save for in the Jewish cemetery. Even there, the untended ancient gravestones are overgrown and difficult to read.

Of course, it is not merely the wiping of historical references and buildings that has been undertaken. On 3rd November 1941, the area was under Nazi occupation. One thousand, five hundred and thirty-five Jews were murdered in Lazdijai: 485 men, 511 women and 539 children. That massacre included almost all the Jews of the tiny *shtetl* of Rudamina. The perpetrators were not Nazis, rather members of the Rollkommando Hamann, local policemen and Lithuanian nationalists. Nowadays, only a handful of Jews remain. Little is left to remind them of better times or even the horrific ones. Except, that is, for the markings on the mass grave at Vichy, and their own memories, many of which are now carefully documented.

Geoff and Gary wondered aimlessly the streets and the surrounding roads. They visited the Jewish graveyard and found the mass grave in the forest. It was a surreal experience. Somehow the holocaust became a personal thing. Of course, they had always found it abhorrent but now they realised that they may have had family directly involved. They were thankful that the Manchester Karavitches had at least escaped that dreadful fate. They were satisfied to breathe the pine-perfumed air of Rudamina, to remember the story that had by a circuitous route eventually produced them, and to give thanks, at least to Harris and Rosa, for their courage and determination. How they wished they could have known them all better! At the small Jewish cemetery, amid the moss-covered graves, the bracken and the weeds, Geoff bent down and picked up a handful of stones to take home with him. A little bit of Rudamina to keep. It was the only souvenir he needed or wanted. His family archaeology had reached a conclusion, at least, until there was another mystery to solve. Fortunately, a few stones wouldn't add too much to his economy flight bag but they would mean a lot to him.

15

Hull: deep and muddy, but land nevertheless

A. D. Mills' *Dictionary of Place Names* gives two lexical meanings for the word 'Hull'. Maybe it is derived from *hul*: from Old Scandinavian 'deep one' or alternatively Celtic 'muddy one' (Mills, 2011) which could be ascribed to the river at a glance on any given day, as an extension of the still-mud-brown and still-deep Humber.

They seem to have dropped the 'Kingston' bit these days.

Perhaps at least that is honest.

The Celts had it right with the mud.

Yet, this was a first step to freedom for many.

Freedom, like gold, can often be found among grime and dirt.

If you look hard enough.

'From Hull, Hell and Halifax, Good Lord deliver us!' someone once said was the thief's plea, to be spared punishment offered in those places. Perhaps all three were too close to the centres of capital punishment at the time. Such a phrase does nothing for Hull Tourist Board. It would, however, take more than winning a City of Culture label or a new marketing slogan (see the mug with 'Hull is not sh-t any more' blazoned on its side) to persuade Geoff that the city was not on its uppers. The weather didn't help, a miserable grey day of drizzle and low cloud that gave way to an early sad sunset, dark at just after 3.30pm. Neither did the road signage nor the parking help. It was probably the roadworks that made them drive round in infuriating circles. Still, once they had parked and had a quick lunch, they could head off to the Museum Quarter. He was in search of more information about the Wilson Shipping Line. Based in Hull, in the late nineteenth century it became the largest shipping line in the world. With its partnership with the Union Castle Line and Northern Railways, it shipped more than wood and raw materials into the wide and ample river mouth that, when the tide was out, slapped with deep mud. Much of its cargo was human, much of that was made up of Jews escaping the Baltic states. Just maybe it was here that the Karavitches landed, here with hundreds of others who were loaded onto trains for Liverpool and then on to who knows where. He knew that many, including Chaim's sons, mistook Hull for New York in *Goldene Medina*, the dream city of most Lithuanian Jews of the time. At least those who had dared to make the treacherous crossing. Perhaps that was easier to do in a world where images were hard to come by and even the alphabet was hard to understand. Certainly, it would have been grander and bigger than any other town they had seen back home. But surely it would have been drably disappointing, too. And many would have missed the open green fields, the blue lakes and dark hills that surrounded their villages.

Geoff imagined for a moment what it might have been like when they came up for air from the depths of the crowded, vomit-strewn steerage. For more than four days, they had been kept like animals in the dark undercarriage of the boats, fed – at best – some bread, gruel and dirty water. They would have been thrown about by each swell. Fighting for enough space and straw to lie on, they had wallowed in vomit and human sweat. Then with a gasp of industrial air, they were greeted by Hull.

'From Hull, Hell and Halifax, Good Lord deliver us!'

Geoff couldn't begin to imagine their experience but he now knew a little of the disappointment that Hull could bring. Yet, to be fair, the approach along the Humber River revealed a wide expansive skyline that graced the magnificent Humber Bridge, and a low setting sun glistening on the water offered some compensation. Sadly, the town remained dismally unforgiving. Roadworks and building sites suggested there were, at present, attempts to improve the centre. There were some beautiful buildings but they seemed to be disguised by the closed shop shutters and the graffiti. Just to add pain to the wound, the very fine Maritime Museum, looking sparkling, even golden, and spanking clean, was sadly still closed, and would be for at least another two years. So nowhere could be found to expand and flesh-out online accounts of Hull's distinguished shipping history. Better, and more pleasant, to raid Wikipedia than to search in Hull, and you could save the parking chaos. Geoff felt somewhat cheated of his expectations. Perhaps, though, not as much as his forbears would have been when they stepped on to the muddy quayside. Thankfully the local Jewish Relief Society was there to offer them some comfort, some food and directions for the next part of their trip.

At least for Geoff on his visit, the Wilberforce Museum was open, and free to enter, though it added little to his family research and they shared the visit with a group of older teenagers let loose only to vape and horseplay among the museum's often distressing contents. Staring at the chains and collar locks, Geoff mused that perhaps even his forbears had not had it that bad. But those forbears were nineteenth-century boat people, whatever the case, humans trying to avoid a different expression of slavery. They have plenty of successors on the coast today. God help them.

Between 1850 and 1914, over two million refugees passed through Hull from the Baltic States. They were mainly Jews from the Russian Empire escaping poverty, pogroms and, in some cases, conscription. That is the negative framing but most were hoping for a brighter, safer future where they would be free to live lives that were productive. Geoff might have been feeling negative about his Hull experience, but the city had a proud shipping history, a proud heritage of supporting the oppressed, and a small compassionate Jewish community. These three elements had combined to form a welcome committee that fed the bedraggled arrivals and helped them board trains to Liverpool.

In those days, Paul Julius Drasdo, a non-Jew of German extraction, was in charge of the landing arrangements. His son gave the following interview: 'The emigrants came across to Hull in the most deplorable conditions. The Russians and the Poles were the majority of the emigrant trade. It was pitiful to see the state they arrived in, and they were herded over here in ships that never should have been allowed to carry passengers. They slept on straw pallets which the crew threw overboard as they were steaming up the Humber River. They were very frightened people. The ship would dock at either the Albert Dock, the Riverside Quay or Victoria Dock, then they would walk to the Paragon Station of the North Eastern Railway where the Emigrant Hall was. This was the reception centre they were all taken to. They would be given a meal – we had a special Kosher kitchen for all the Jewish passengers, who were segregated from the Christians. The Jewish kitchen was looked after by the local Jewish residents of Hull, who were wonderfully helpful even though they didn't know the emigrants from Adam.'

Mr Drasdo's first job was to inspect them, check for illness and to generally vet them. Then they were grouped and taken to the waiting trains that had been organised. These trains took the emigrants (those wanting to get to the USA or Canada) to Liverpool, and those who had decided to settle in the UK: usually Dublin, Leeds or Manchester.[1]

Among them, Geoff knew, he could feel it in his waters, even in the rain, were the Karavitches, his paternal forbears: Isaac and Abraham, Woolf, and of course his great-granddad Harris. For many young couples like them, this was the first land they saw beyond the Pale. This is where the fresh steps to a future began, a future that eventually produced Geoff ... and Linda, Brian and Gary, of course. This is where the Wilson Line would have provided them with seamless travel to 'Cottonopolis'.

---

[1] Quoted in Sugarman Philip, Hull, England, Jewish Virtual Library, 2005

16

Call me by a name, any name you like

A name is a word or phrase that constitutes the distinctive designation of a person or thing.

You have to be called something.

You have no choice

'No Name' is not an option even though

for some people that is exactly how they feel.

There are regimes who have used numbers instead of names.

They were trying to remove

any ounce of humanity that was left.

But in truth you are more than a number

or a name.

Geoff followed the seamless route to Manchester but not on the Northern Railway Line (which had long since changed hands and brands) or indeed any transport departing from Hull. The city greeted him with rain, but he had expected nothing else. It helped him know he was home. That and the Co-op Insurance tower just near Victoria Station. Yet the strange thing is, seen through Karavitch eyes, the city felt alien, remote and unexplored. Funny, he realised perhaps for the first time, that the city of your birth is smaller than you would admit. At least your perception of that city. You tended to know the housing estate where you lived, the shopping centre you shopped at, the parks you played in. Then, perhaps, the town centre itself, your favourite stores, the railway stations, the pubs and clubs of your youthful energies. But what about the rest? He remembered visiting Mary Ellen and Pa in Moss Side with his mum, but so much of it had been bull-dozed, cleared with the slums in the 1970s. So, in a real way he was about to discover his own city, or to be more precise, discover some of the city of the Karavitches. How had it looked, and felt, to them?

Even today the tall, grim tower of Strangeways Prison (now Manchester Prison) dominates the neighbourhood of what was the Karavitches' first home. Berkley Street, however, has long since gone, and only a remnant of Julia Street retains a meagre existence. The prison stands firm, arrogantly proud. Its construction was completed in 1868, some twenty years before Harris and Rosa arrived. Designed by Alfred Waterhouse, this huge monolith was built in brick and sandstone. As a child, he always presumed that the phallic-like tower was to keep watch over dangerous prisoners headstrong on escape. Now he knew that it formed part of the ventilation and heating system. The minaret-style tower could hold its own on any number of eastern city landscapes, save for its sooty grime and the constant rain. He found it frightening as a child; perhaps that was its secondary purpose: a design to deter would-be criminals of all kinds. It must have been especially so to Simon and his street friends as they played their games on crowded cobbled streets in its shadow. There are almost no houses in the neighbourhood now. Merely run-down businesses. Car body-shops and clothing warehouses are two-a-penny. By all accounts, however, it was a flourishing neighbourhood at the turn of the twentieth century. The famous Boddington's Brewery (demolished in 2007), the Weatherproof Garment Factories such as Cohen and Wilkes in Derby Street, Bloom Brothers in North Street, and the iron and brick works which darkened the riverside area, bringing work, grime, noise and people. Nestled in between the industrial sites were thriving clusters of over-full, busy terraced houses. Small shops dotted about, serving the resident population, most of whom came from Eastern Europe in various waves of immigration. It is hard to believe that until the 19th century, this was a rural village dominated by Strangeways Hall, Park and Gardens. Today, as in Simon's time, there are no grass or trees in sight. Berkley Street might have been prosperous once, but the arrival of Eastern bloc Jews, at the turn of the century, brought it down a peg or two. Especially compared to Moreton Street, where rents were higher. Where Berkley Street intersected Julia Street, there was a popular bakery, dairy and 'sell-you-anything' shop run by Mrs Cohen and her children. The children could be seen carrying an urn of milk to the prison early every morning while Mrs Cohen made her bakery deliveries to regular customers. The knocker-up man paraded the streets at dawn, rousing sleepy-eyed, tired men for prayers. It was the only way they could ensure a *minyan* (the number of men needed for a synagogue to meet, which was ten). Hob-nail boots would scrape the cobbles as the factory shifts began, leaving the women to their daily chores. Steps were cleared and carpets beaten, baking and washing had their set days. But the kids played, as kids do, often reworking traditional English street games that they only half understood. 'Who was May Pole?' a child asked as she danced. She was thinking May might live on Rosamund Street or in some distant neighbourhood!

Here, immigrants learnt a new language, here, they adapted the songs and the games to suit old family traditions that their parents taught them. Though their families came from different parts of the

Russian Empire, they shared much, speaking Yiddish at home and attending *cheder* (school) together, learning Hebrew, the boys preparing for *bar-mitzvah*. Small *minyans* met in houses to worship but larger synagogues soon developed with every tradition and nuance. Harris and Rose would have found friends from back home living close by, perhaps especially in the Kovno Synagogue in Moreton Street. Today, the oldest synagogue left is no longer in use; instead, it forms part of a Jewish Museum. It is Sephardic. Simon would probably have known it well. But the Karavitches, like the majority of Eastern bloc immigrants, were Ashkenazi, and would have worshipped elsewhere. Rosenburg's butcher was busy on Bury New Road, as was Glasky's bakehouse and, of course, Needhof's bakery. There were schools on every corner and on Sunday mornings, under the bridge, stalls sold rags and textile seconds. Perhaps it was there that Woolfe and Harris began trading themselves. This tight-knit, ever-expanding 'foreign Manchester' was where Simon, his brothers and sisters grew up. Here they went to school, played and began their working lives. It is easy to imagine Simon on his bike, an errand boy, before he learnt the family trade of 'scissors and ironing board.' The Karavitches did not seem destined to join the *reich* (rich) but they slowly made a more prosperous life for themselves. Before long, they moved to Moss Lane, a typical move south for this community. Slowly, they became more stable financially, more settled into English life, scrambling their way out of poverty. Here, they began their selling of rags and fents (textile seconds), perhaps on Sundays under those arches, but eventually in their own shop and warehouse. Manchester had for them become home.

Naming people and animals (and probably things, too) is perhaps a quintessential (even sacred) human activity. We are told as such in the ancient book of Genesis, when in the Garden of Eden, God gives the naming task to the humans he has just created. Until we learn animal talk, we will never know if other creatures have their own way of marking or identifying fellow creatures. Perhaps they work better with smells or with acute observation that clocks differences in movements and actions. It looks that way on wildlife documentaries. But do they give or use names? Names seem to be a human practice, the result of language skills. Ancients, however, believed that to know someone's name was to have a certain power over that person. Hence, the scandal of the story of Moses learning the name of God at the burning bush: Yahweh (*I am*). Hence, the refusal of a faithful Jew to write or say the name of G-d. More simply, school teachers know the power of knowing a name: shout, 'Quiet!' to a class of children and they often (mostly) carry on talking, shout, 'Be quiet, Jonny!' and Jonny usually obeys. (Experience says it is sometimes useful to have a handful of kids called Jonny in the same class, though to be fair it wouldn't guarantee a quiet class.) Or walk into a party, bubbling with chatter, and you will hear your own name when spoken from across the other side of the buffet. Immediately it demands your attention.

Fashion and purpose in naming changes all the time. Old family traditions were to call your children after their forebears, to carry on the family name. Nowadays, British parents often do the exact opposite; they desire a 'unique' name for their child, which if nothing else is a reminder that each person is unique. Hirsch and Rosa had adapted their names to signal the beginning of a new life. Simon Karavitch believed that in changing his name he could become someone different, but it was an illusion that never became a reality. Harold Miller could not change how he was known, how he felt about himself. He would always be Harold Miller, despite a birth certificate giving him a different name. Geoff never lived to become a star of Hollywood westerns but maybe he learnt something about being God-fearing, not too much, mind. Perhaps, at best, a name is either descriptive or aspirational. Married women, who accept a new family name on their wedding day, could give us all a lesson in name changing. How do they cope with the change? How does it make them feel? Of course, it doesn't change who they are, merely who they might become. No wonder a growing number reject the change and opt for an equal approach to a change of status, a common partnership for the future. A double-barrel alternative. Maybe the best you can hope for is to grow into your name. So, choosing a first name for a child is a kind of hope or prayer for what that child might become. Or, maybe, it might be useful if everybody had a few names up their sleeves to interchange at any point for the different people they want to be at that moment in time ...

Geoff and his brother Gary (*Gary* – 'spear'/sharp) arrived at the cemetery to find what was left of Simon Israel Karavitch, the grandfather they never knew. It was a cemetery full of simple, dignified though aging gravestones. Most were covered in algae with eroding lettering and advancing green moss. Geoff and Gary, ironically both Christian priests, were not new to gravesides and headstones but they were immediately struck with a cultural difference. Simple, almost uniform headstones, marked in Hebrew, so difficult for them to decipher and read. Unlike the Christian and secular sections nearby, there were no flowers placed at gravesides. Jewish graves do not crave dying, rotting 'signs of life' even if they were once pretty in full bloom. Rather, they prefer stones placed upon them. Markers of a visit to pay respect, a solid sign of perpetual memory.

It is impossible to rewrite history. Of course, you can try, and many have, but failure is sure. The present is yours – *that* you can change. That is within your power, if only you have the desire and the courage. But can you redeem the past, can you right wrongs, put things right? In truth, probably not, but maybe it is worth a try. I suppose it depends on which past you want to redeem, whose stories you want to retell.

*

Joe Daniels had disappeared into the mists of unreal history. Simon Karavitch, however, remained, broken to be sure, but though head down, he lived on. He wanted most of all to disappear into the background, to just quietly exist, to forget his adolescent foolishness. Except of course for Maurice. He was the only good thing to have survived that painful episode. Simon had made a life post Mary Ellen. Nathan was his best support, and *Mame*, of course. He had caused enough humiliation to last more than a lifetime, for him and all of the

Karavitches. He carried on working at the warehouse for a while. When Nathan took over his father-in-law's fruit and fish shop, he asked Simon to join him. Nathan, possibly like his namesake the biblical prophet, had a heart for the underdog. He cared for his older brother, gave him a fresh start. There he stayed for the rest of an uneventful life. That's how he wanted it. He had had all the adventure he could cope with, all the disappointment he could take. It was more than enough for him and he lived with only one regret: never again to hear his lad call him *Abba*. But he remembered those early-formed baby sounds, that weak fist-wave as, leaning on her shoulder, Mary Ellen carried him away. Calling it to mind was still painful, always it would bring another tear to his deep, dark eyes, another tear to hide from the two worlds that he had failed so miserably to navigate. He could forget so much: the flamboyant, brassy, lipstick-painted girl who had captured him so easily; the rapture of a romance and a fulfilled young man's misdirected dreams; the betrayal of knowing that you have been played with and discarded; the fear of hatred and the drudgery of a life without meaning. But he couldn't forget the purple, scrawny, crying prune-like baby with the piercing eyes and the mop of black hair. Maurice, his son. The only good, perfect, beautiful thing he had produced.

*

The Jewish Cemetery in Blackley was not hard to find but it was quite a task to gain entry. Geoff and Gary drove around at first; they could see the graves but couldn't find the way in. By chance they spotted a gateway off the busy road, then realised with a sigh that it was a locked. A notice pinned to the gate gave a phone number which put them in touch with a friendly voice who offered them a secret access code. That was the easy bit! They were then faced with hundreds of gravestones, tightly packed together. Trying to walk respectfully among them was hazardous. Unlike the cemeteries Gary and Geoff were used to, there were no family plots. They struggled. Another phone call to the friendly volunteer revealed that people were buried in order, in the next grave available. The guide told them that the graves should be better located by date, so to speak.

'Follow the dates,' he said, 'and that should get you to the spot.'

It was like a clue in an escape room challenge. Then the guide gently warned us that Jewish order can sometimes go awry.

'Keep looking,' he said. 'It doesn't get dark for quite a while yet. Though I hope you have brought sandwiches.'

Intrepid to the end, Gary and Geoff found the headstones of Woolf and Dora first, then Harris and Rose, even though the carved letters were blurred by age and in Hebrew. They paused at each one, just for moment, enough to remember that these were their unknown forbears, and to give thanks. However, it took the help of a photograph to find the headstone that declared 'Simon Israel Karavitch'. Unsurprisingly as they read the translated inscription, there was no reference to Joe Daniels. But in all honesty that wasn't the disturbing omission. The carving read:

In Loving Memory of

SIMON KAYE KARAVITCH

Died 8 May 1964 aged 70 years

Deeply mourned by his brother,

Sisters, brother-in-law, nephews

Nieces, relatives and friends,

And sister-in-law.

M.H.D.S. R.I.P.

No mention of Maurice, Simon's son, no reference to Simon as a father. That piece of his history had been obliterated, erased, deleted. According to his headstone, Simon had no son, no male offspring, to pray *kaddish* at his graveside. Would he have objected, shouted from his plain coffin, 'Maurice called me *Abba*, he did, he did!'? Or perhaps, he too, had erased Maurice along with Joe? Mary Ellen had certainly acquiesced to such sentiment. She had raised a

Harold not a Maurice, after all. Maurice would have mourned Simon if he had had the chance, because Harold mourned him all his life. But remember you can't change history; try as you may, you can't rewrite the past. That was beyond even Mary Ellen's powers. You could change a name, even destroy a body, but not erase a birth or a life. Neither can you correct history, I suppose. But there again death does not respect time, for time is but a human construct.

Geoff took the three stones he had carried from Rudamina out of his bag. A trinity of stones, one for each bottle of vodka, the spirits that had saved his family so many years ago. One for Gary, one for himself and one to keep just in case it was needed. He remembered old Nathan's good advice. He also took out his beautifully embroidered Jewish prayer shawl. It was a precious gift given to him by friends when he was on pilgrimage to Jerusalem. He ran his hand softly over its silken, striped cloth. His fingers separated, nervously playing with the delicate fringes and knots. He called to mind the story that had begun in the tiny village on the Lithuanian Polish border, near Suwałki. In his mind's eye he watched the merriment and the dancing on a wedding day; he felt the fear of hatred, of thrown stones, of broken glass and bones, and the wild threatening of heavy sticks; he witnessed the night-time torches, the grand procession and the grave decision made amid the joy of Simchat Torah; he envisaged the treacherous journeys full of terror, vomit and hope, and the long hours of drudgery that followed to build a new life; he watched the young scrawny errand boy on his bike delivering groceries to frail old ladies. Then the same lad working with scissors and ironing board, the apprentice learning his trade. The alluring glances amid bails of cloth, and of course the stray football in the park. The reckless leaving, the anger of some, as well as the gentle welcoming of others. Most of all he was haunted by the tiny baby with black staring eyes looking over its mother's shoulder mouthing *Abba* and coyly waving a good bye. This could not be erased, it could not be forgotten and Geoff was proof of its enduring presence.

He would not wear the shawl, he could not, should not, but he would place it on his shoulder. He had no right to call himself Jewish.

Like his brother, he was a Christian priest. That indeed was a different story for a different time. Now he was standing at this Hebrew grave, the grave that belonged to his grandfather: the *Saba* he never knew. Now along with his brother, they would offer what he, and Gary, alone could offer, the responsibility of the closest male relatives to Simon Israel. They each placed their Rudaminian pebble on the top of the aging gravestone, bringing a journey to its full circle. The third pebble Geoff put back in his pocket; maybe his son would find a use for it in time to come. Together in hushed, sombre tones they began to recite the mourner's prayer, the *Kaddish*:

Exalted and hallowed be God's great name
in the world which God created, according to plan.
May God's majesty be revealed in the days of our lifetime
and the life of all Israel — speedily, imminently,
To which we say: **Amen.**

17

A last word, perhaps

Postscript: text added at the end of a book or other document. 'Postscript' comes from the Latin word *postscribere*, with 'post' meaning 'after' and *scribere* meaning 'to write'.

Who gets the last word in a story,

the story teller?

Or does a story ever end?

Here's to the next story maker.

Take the baton.

It's all yours.

Though there is truth in this account, to be honest, for once at least, it is not found in abundance. The facts are there in names and dates, but there is little truth to be found in the drawing of characters and creating of their stories. Much of what you have read is the product of an over-active imagination. More worryingly, some of the cast are its victims. What is definitely true is the answer to the question, 'Who is Joe Daniels?' He certainly is (or was) Simon Israel Karavitch, son of Harris and Rose Karavitch. Most of the rest of his story, as recounted in these pages, is pure imagination, except of course Joe's marriage to Mary Ellen and their son Maurice or Harold – take your pick which name best suits the child. For those who concern themselves with fact, what some call truth, you will have to do your own research, or use your own discernment, to make a judgement. I'll stick with Pontius Pilate and see the question, 'What is truth?' as an impossible one to (dare we say, *truthfully*) answer.

When it comes to Mary Ellen and Hal's story, we are on safer ground. It's certainly true, at least to Geoff and his family, that Mary Ellen was a difficult matriarch with great manipulation, disruption and control skills. Quite why she worked that way is a mystery. Many families of the time experienced such devious matriarchs. Did society make them, or was it in their genes? Were they just one particular way in which communities bound families together or downtrodden women refused to be silenced or disabled? Geoff remembers Mary Ellen distinctly, with a shudder and yet a strange affection. Without her, this story would be pretty mundane. It is a pity, perhaps, that she would never spill the beans about Joe. However, if she had, it may have described events unworthy of writing up, so that is something for which to be grateful. Most of all, by far, it is her father, Jack Ellis, who comes off worse in these pages. He is a true victim. He isn't around to give his own account and any suggestion he was a cruel, fist-throwing drunkard is more a projection on the writer's part. More than likely, he was absolutely nothing of the sort, and therefore, God forbid that what is written here should be his epithet. Profound apologies, Jack. But then what drove Mary Ellen? How was the matriarch made? If Jack Ellis wasn't to blame (and he probably wasn't), then was there some other cause that could be identified, save for a malevolence all of her own? How he wished he could ask her! But he guessed she wouldn't have answered.

Camels' posteriors and sandstorms come to mind.

ABOUT THE AUTHOR

Geoff Miller is the former Dean of Newcastle. Married to Elaine, he has one son, Philip. He spent 40 years living and working in the North East of England, and is now retired and living in Newcastle. However, he still considers himself a Mancunian and recollects Wythenshawe with some deep affection.

ACKNOWLEDGEMENTS

There are too many sources to list but grateful thanks to Jan Harney, as always, you are my go-to encourager. Brenda and Brian Dinsdale for a lovely Shabbat meal and great advice. Stuart Rosenblatt of the Irish Jewish Genealogical Society. The Manchester Jewish Museum, and the Manchester Police Museum. A host of books and websites but especially JewGen.org and its Lithuanian sections.

And of course, to my brother Gary, and to Flip, the heir apparent. Finally, to Elaine who I shamelessly tricked by promising not to write a sequel to 'Who is Joe Daniels?' but started on the prequel instead. Elaine, I make no promises this time.

Printed in Dunstable, United Kingdom

64839622R00087